D0007949

cycler

Lauren McLaughlin

Random House New York

This is a work of fiction. Names, characters, places, and incidents either are the product of the author's imagination or are used fictitiously. Any resemblance to actual persons, living or dead, events, or locales is entirely coincidental.

 Published in the United States by Random House Children's Books, a division of Random House, Inc., New York.

Random House and colophon are registered trademarks of Random House, Inc.

Visit us on the Web! www.randomhouse.com/teens

Educators and librarians, for a variety of teaching tools, visit us at www.randomhouse.com/teachers

Library of Congress Cataloging-in-Publication Data
McLaughlin, Lauren.
Cycler / by Lauren McLaughlin. — 1st ed.
p. cm.
Summary: Seventeen-year-old Jill is a fairly normal high school senior whose focus is on getting a certain boy to ask her to prom, but four days a month she transforms into surly Jack, who decides it is time he had his own life and a chance with the girl he wants.
ISBN 978-0-375-85191-9 (trade) — ISBN 978-0-375-95191-6 (lib. bdg.)
[1. Sex—Fiction. 2. Interpersonal relations—Fiction. 3. Family problems—Fiction. 4. High schools—Fiction. 5. Schools—Fiction. 6. Massachusetts—Fiction.] I. Title.
PZ7.M2238Cyc 2008
[Fic]—dc22 2007042304

Printed in the United States of America

10 9 8 7 6 5 4 3 2 1

First Edition

For Carol and Tom McLaughlin

February 16

Jill

"I am all girl."

It's my own voice I hear as I lie in bed half-awake, half-asleep. In my dream, I'm walking barefoot through the woods behind my house. It's fall, and the flame-colored leaves float softly downward. Out of nowhere, a Ferris wheel appears and I get on without a ticket.

"I am all girl."

I say it because my body is betraying me.

In my dream, the colorful autumn day becomes night. The Ferris wheel speeds up, breaks free of its foundation and rolls through the darkened woods. Shearing tree branches with loud splintery crunches, it rolls toward the black lake at the edge of the tree line.

From deep within me, behind organs, beneath muscles, a jagged pain is born.

"I am all girl!"

I open my eyes to the real night, the thick molasses darkness of it. But it's only when I spot the red numbers of my clock that I'm sure I'm awake: 4:27 a.m. The pain is building to a sure and steady climax and I don't know who I am.

Jack or Jill.

"I am all girl!" I squeeze through clenched teeth.

There's a land mine exploding outward from my stomach and lower spine.

I'm not supposed to wake up in the middle of things. All of this is supposed to happen while I sleep. I shove my hand beneath the sheets, praying, hoping the transformation is nearly complete, but when I reach lower, there it is—limp, smooth and insistent.

Jack.

He's supposed to fade in the night and I'm supposed to wake up fully constructed. Instead, I have his *thing* to contend with and a deep ache that, now that I think of it, is not exploding outward but sucking inward like a vortex.

"I am all girl."

That's my mantra. I use it to forget. But it does nothing to ease the pain.

The muscles of my abdomen spasm and I squeeze Jack's thing in response, as if he were doing this to me—the sadistic jerk. I know that's not true. Grabbing the pillow with my other hand, I press it to my face.

"I am all girl," I growl. I don't want to scream, but I can't stop myself.

"I . . . !"

I'm lost now, a rudderless ship on a wild and cruel ocean.

"Mom!"

I know she can't help. No one can.

"Mom!"

The bedroom door opens; then the bed sags with Mom's weight. Her perfect brown bob is sleep-mussed and her pale face bears deep pillow wrinkles.

"Shhh," she says. "It's okay, honey. 'I am all girl.' Say it."

"I am all girl."

I want to absorb relief from these words or from the forced calm of my mother's face, but relief never comes. Looking past her, I spot Dad hovering in the doorway, disheveled as always and chewing on his thumbnail. No relief there either.

Then the split begins.

At the base of Jack's thing, the pain gathers to a diamond point. I grab Mom's cool hand and squeeze. My flesh punctures from within. Then, zipperlike, it tears itself open. I throw my head from side to side.

"I." Gasp. "Am." Gasp. "All." Gasp. "Girl!"

"It's okay," Mom says. But I hear the strain in her voice. She's starting to panic too.

The split now complete beneath Jack's quivering thing, I try to pull my legs together. I don't know why. Protective instinct, I guess. But I can't control my legs or anything else. My body is in control, orchestrating its mal proceedings from the angry vortex at the base of my spine.

The vortex sucks harder now, pulling at my bones, my muscles, retracting my thighs, melting the firm stomach until it's soft and feminine. My body remakes itself with no mercy, sanding the crisp edges from my jawbone, deflating the gentle biceps, brutally inflating my breasts.

"I am all girl!" I scream, all sense gone.

"Shhh," Mom says. "Breathe, baby."

But every breath is a new gut wound. The bones of my ankles rearrange themselves in miniature. Even my toes protest the change. Unthinkingly, I clench Jack's thing with my sweaty hand and force the breath out in an angry rhythm.

"That's right," Mom says. "Breathe."

With what's left of my brain, I can still remember, I can still think. Jackthoughts, Jackfears, Jackdesires. He's angry. At me. At Mom. He doesn't like chunky peanut butter and she keeps feeding it to him. He wants a new pair of boxer briefs and some Elvis DVDs. He wants us to turn the Internet back on.

"I am all girl!"

I clench Jack's thing harder now and it slips weakly from my slick palm into the sucking mouth of the vortex.

And then it's gone.

All of it.

Not just Jack, but the pain too. That's the merciful afterthought of this wicked hullabaloo. The pain doesn't fade slowly the way it builds. It evaporates in a euphoric instant.

I look up at Mom's ever-calm face backlit from the hall light spilling through the open door. She whisks a strand of hair from her eyes, then touches my cheek with the backs of her fingers. "Plan B?" she says.

"Not now," I say. "Too tired."

I lift my head to look at Dad. His greasy hair and guru beard connect in a continuous circle of grunge around his frightened face. He's the same mess he has been for years. But I'm so blissed out on post-agony, I can't help but love the guy.

"Sorry, Dad," I say.

"It's okay, honey."

But he's still chewing on his thumbnail because it's not okay and he knows it. It's never going to be okay either. Not for him, not for me. Not for any member of the McTeague household.

Within this house is a monster, a freak, a slave to the calendar and my own lunatic hormones. Before every menstrual cycle—every phase of the moon, if you want to be romantic about it—I am savagely transformed from girl to boy for four full days, then wickedly reshaped into girlflesh again. Most of the time, I sleep right through it. Most of the time.

"Good night," I say. "I'll do Plan B in the morning."

Within seconds, I'm out.

Four and a half hours later, my eyes open to the bleak February light straining to pass through my bedroom's frosty windows. Sinking low beneath the down comforter, I cocoon myself for an extra moment. But when dim memories of the night before begin to intrude, I peel the comforter back and begin the rituals of Plan B.

Not the contraceptive, dummy. Believe me, if I could have prevented Jack's conception, I would have been all over that. Plan B is my four-step method for minimizing the overall malness of his existence.

The first step is to fix an image of my female face in my mind's eye. I do this by sitting upright in bed and facing the mirror above my dresser. I stare at my too-small eyes, my wide cheeks. I am not beautiful, but that's not the point. I am female. That's what matters. Straining to banish judgment, I absorb the image.

In Step Two, I lie down, close my eyes and begin my mantra: "I am all girl." Silently, I repeat the phrase in time with my breathing. It's like this: Breathe in, think: *I am.* Breathe out, think: *all girl.* Meanwhile, I envision a black dot in the center of my forehead. That's the third eye. If I maintain focus and calm, the black dot inflates like a balloon until it engulfs my whole head. That's the meditative state.

In Step Three, I project Jack's four days onto the blackness as if it were a giant movie. Then, before I can absorb any of the details, I make the image fade to black.

In Step Four, I paste the mirror image of my own face onto the blackness. It's dim at first, but as I repeat the mantra in rhythm with my breathing, it sharpens and brightens until I see a crystal clear image of my imperfect female face. At that moment, I know it's safe to open my eyes. Whatever transpired during Jacktime is erased, forgotten, swallowed up by the vortex with his limp thing. That's Plan B. Pretty brilliant, huh?

Sitting up on the bed, I take a big disgusting whiff of myself, then head straight for the shower. Jack doesn't bathe. I wrote him a note about it once and he wrote back that since he has to endure *my* PMS for the duration of his phase, I should cut him some slack on hygiene. I guess that makes sense in boy logic. I run the shower hot and steamy, then lather up to begin the de-stinkification.

I'm not saying I'm a genius or anything, but you have to admit that Plan B is a deeply non-dumb invention. We cobbled it together after the nightmare transformations began at the tender age of fourteen. By "we," I mean mostly me and my mom. Dad had already begun his slide into that mal universe of yoga, hair growth and transcendental meditation he now occupies from his headquarters in our basement. But that's another story. You know what Dad's initial response to my crisis was? "Let's all meditate toward acceptance."

Acceptance schmacceptance. If you're blind, you can talk about acceptance. If you're deaf or paraplegic or have any number of comparably tolerable conditions, you can talk about acceptance. What I have is not acceptable.

Nor is this oil slick masquerading as my hair. Jack takes greasy to a new level. I squirt out half a bottle of shampoo and let it sit on my head as I shave my stubbly legs. I have four full days of neglect to deal with in here.

So anyway, back to Plan B. Medical science had nothing to say on the subject of my bewildering condition, so when the gazillionth hospital visit resulted in yet another round of incredulous stares from a roomful of medical skeptics, Mom and I decided to do our own research. We spent hours and days and weeks and months online and at the library. We read medical journals written in jargon so technical you had to read other books just to understand them. We learned so much about the human body, we could have performed open-heart surgery on each other. And you know what the grand conclusion of all this research was? "You're on your own, sweetheart."

Those were dark days, I can tell you. Dad had moved into the basement by then. Mom was experimenting with estrogen therapy. On herself! And I was hiding out in my room lest anyone discover the mortifying truth about my cyclical "condition."

Then one day, while spiraling down the Google rabbit hole, I stumbled on a Web site for people who use self-hypnosis to erase painful memories.

My wheels started turning.

You see, we'd already decided to hide my condition from the outside world when it became clear that medical science was basically useless. Mom even went to the principal of Winterhead High with a phony doctor's note and a story about how I needed blood transfusions every four weeks for a severe iron deficiency, thus smoothing over my periodic absences from school. I figured since we were obliterating the condition from the public record, why not obliterate it from my own memory? I'll admit, it was a crazy idea, as evidenced by the fact that it drew Dad out of his basement yoga hole to donate his newfound expertise on transcendental meditation. Oddly enough, it was the perfect addition. He even came up with the mantra "I am all girl."

I've been doing Plan B for three years now, and it works so well I no longer have any recollection of my days as a boy. It's like hitting the delete button on my memory. Bam! Four days disappear.

Told you it was brilliant.

As I step from the shower into the warm embrace of a clean white towel, I am smooth, degreased and stink free.

I stand in front of my overstuffed closet to wait for inspiration. Per usual, I've woken up with my period, so I select my extra stretchy black jeans. Then I add a white lace top and a burgundy velvet jacket. I'm about to head downstairs for breakfast when I remember a critical incident from the day before Jack arrived. It happened in chem lab.

Mom knocks on the door. "French toast's ready."

She always makes French toast on my first day back.

"Wait, Mom." I open the door. "Cell phone?"

She removes it from the front pocket of her beige pants. "We should just have this thing fastened to the side of your face, you know."

"Funny." I take it from her and close the door. Then I call my best friend, Ramie. She picks up on the second ring.

"I need your advice," I tell her.

"It's Saturday," she says. "Do I have to be wise?"

"I'll settle for non-dumb," I say. "When can you get here?"

"Depends."

"On?"

"On whether I can excavate your closet," she says. "I'm working on some new ideas."

When Ramie says "new ideas," start worrying. She's obsessed with fashion. Not "mindless status fashion," as she calls it, but "serious editorial fashion," whatever that is. She once came to school wearing her father's gray business suit *underneath* a 1940s vintage swimsuit. That's Ramie.

"Deal," I say. "Just get here."

Ramie arrives half an hour later and rips me away from the remains of my French toast. She's armed with a stack of Italian *Vogues*, so we head straight up to my room. I love when my first day back falls on a Saturday so I can spend some quality girl time with Ramie. It's like pounding one final nail into Jack's coffin.

Spreading the magazines out on my bed, she sits among them and starts flipping through the November issue. Without looking up, she says, "Treatments go okay?"

"Piece of cake," I say. The "treatments" are my fictional blood transfusions. Ramie stopped pumping me for details about them when I told her I did not want to be "defined by my illness."

After a round of furious page flipping, Ramie looks up from her magazine and evaluates my outfit. "You need to rethink that jacket," she says.

I smooth my hands over the velvet jacket, which fits me like a glove, then have a look in the mirror above the dresser. "Why? It's deeply flattering."

"It's too fitted." She lies on her stomach and eyeballs me while flipping through her magazine at warp speed. "So, what's the deal?" she says.

I sit on the bed and leaf through the June issue. "Well," I say. "It turns out I have a bit of a senior prom issue."

She stops flipping. "How can you have a prom issue? It's only February. Prom isn't for another . . ." She starts counting out the months on her fingers.

"Four months." I point to the calendar above my desk. "One hundred and twenty-six days, to be precise."

Ramie stares at the calendar, on which I've written the remaining days until prom night in every single square. "Uh, Jill," she says. "You need help."

"That's why you're here."

"Dude, I meant professional help." She returns to her magazine. "Ooh, ooh," she says. "Look at this." She slides it across the bed. It's opened to a crazy picture of a model layered with acres of clashing Aztec prints.

"She looks fat," I say.

"It's volume, Jill." She pulls the magazine back to her side of the bed. "Skinny is over. It's all about volume."

"Uh-huh." The only good thing I can say about the picture is that it was shot in the desert. Someplace hot. I hate winter. It dominates so much of the calendar here in Massachusetts, they named my town Winterhead. How depressing is that?

Ramie turns the page slowly to a DPS, which stands for double page spread in the fashion industry. "Now that's what I call styling," she says. Then she peels all five feet ten inches of her fat-free body off the bed and stands before my open closet. She pulls out a white corset dress. Laying it on the bed, she pulls off her cruddy beige sweater, which causes her D-cup boobs to bounce beneath her pink alligator shirt. When I called her "fat free," I forgot to mention the boobs. Ramie's built like a bombshell. She lays the cruddy sweater on top of the white dress and says, "Counterpoint. It's all about counterpoint."

"I thought it was all about volume."

"They're not incompatible, smart-ass." From the back pocket of her baggy jeans, she pulls a wide rainbow-striped ribbon and cinches the sweater at the waist with it. "So, do I have to beat it out of you or are you going to tell me about this prom issue?" She goes to my closet and drops to her knees to excavate the crate of accessories I keep on the floor.

"Okay." I move all the magazines to my desk to make room for her experiment in contrapuntal styling. "So, last week in chem lab," I say, "Steven Price asked me to the prom."

Ramie twists her head over her shoulder to look at me. "Steven Price?"

She looks really pretty when she does that, so I make a mental note of it. It may come in handy later when I need to look alluring. "Yup," I say. "We were washing beakers and he just blurted it out."

Ramie stands up with a giant hair clip and uses it to cinch the waist of the sweater lying on the bed. "Hmm," she says. "You're not secretly in love with Steven Price and about to tell me this is deeply good news, right?"

I slump on the bed next to the outfit. "He's a really, really super nice guy but—"

"You don't have to say it." Ramie bunches up the sleeves of the cruddy beige sweater. "Geeks are deeply cool now, but somehow Steven manages to be just geeky. What did you say?"

"I said, 'Gosh, Steven, don't you think it's a little early for that?' "

"Ouch," Ramie says.

"I know." I tie the beige sweater in a knot at the midriff in an attempt to minimize its influence on the outfit as a whole. "The last thing I want to do is hurt Steven's feelings," I say. "We've been lab partners for two years."

"Uh-huh." She adjusts the ribbon's bow just left of center, then decides against it and rips it off.

"Mom says guys like Steven Price are good to keep track of for later use," I say. "But for right now—social death."

Ramie just stares at me.

"I know. But that's Mom for you. Anyway, the whole sad incident got me thinking about the fact that I have no boyfriend, no prospects and no strategy in place to ensure a successful prom experience."

"Hmm" is all Ramie comes up with. Then she returns to the closet floor, where an ecosystem of forgotten clothes has taken root. I suppose I should mention that Ramie thinks the prom is stupid. Ramie thinks all high school traditions are stupid.

She stands up holding a bright paisley scarf and lays it across the ugly beige sweater. "There." She backs away from the outfit and squints at it. Then she rips off her pink alligator shirt and squeezes her D-cup boobs into the B-cup corset dress. "Zip me," she says.

I get the zipper an inch up her back. "Can you breathe?"

"Nope," she says. "Keep zipping."

She sucks in her stomach and I tug the zipper half an inch higher. "That's it."

I stand back as she pulls on the beige sweater and ties it at the breastbone.

"You have to be willing to suffer for your art," she says.

"Uh-huh."

As fun as it is watching Ramie bust out of my corset dress, I'm distracted by my prom issue. You see, once I started worrying about the prom, a certain someone I had previously not noticed suddenly made himself intriguingly visible to me. It was as if the universe itself were summoning its awesome powers to save me from prom malness.

I take a deep breath. "So, Rames," I say. "What do you think about Tommy Knutson?"

"Tommy Knutson?" she says. "You mean that weird guy from Brazil?" She grabs a pink down vest from my closet.

"New York," I tell her. "I think he moved here from New York."

"Oh. I heard Brazil," she says. "But then I also heard L.A. He's kind of mysterious, right? Doesn't talk much?"

"No," I say. "But he's been doing sticky eyes with me."

"Really?"

"We're in H Block calculus together," I tell her. "He sits one row over and two seats in front of me, and last week he started doing it."

"Uh-huh." She zips the puffy pink vest over the outfit.

"I'm not talking furtive glances either," I say. "I'm talking one Mississippi, two Mississippi, three. Once, I counted all the way to five."

"You count?" She hands me the rainbow ribbon and sticks her arms out to the side. I tie the ribbon around her waist. "Higher," she says. "Empire."

I hike the ribbon up, leaving the puffy down vest to bulge beneath it like a pregnant belly.

"So that's what this is all about?" Ramie says. "You want to go to the prom with Tommy Knutson?"

"Right now I consider him Candidate Number One."

Ramie hands me a white cashmere beret and I tuck her wild black bramble hair into it.

"He *is* non-ugly," she says.

Believe it or not, that's a big statement coming from Ramie. She's given up on guys until she gets to college, where she fully intends to have an affair with a professor. A *European* professor. No, I'm serious. That's her plan.

"Before you commit, though," she says, "let me do some digging."

I panic. "Ramie, you cannot under any circumstances let Tommy Knutson know I have any interest in him."

"Spot me some credit, Jill. I said digging, not blabbing." Ramie turns to the side to evaluate her profile. "Uh, Jill, do you see something wrong with this picture?"

I check out her profile. "Yeah, Rames. You look like a whale."

"Not that, dummy." She points to her beret. "White hat.

White dress. It's too matchy matchy." She rips off the beret and shakes out her wild hair.

"Yeah, Rames. That was the problem with the look. You've definitely nailed it now."

She turns from side to side to examine the full heft of the mal outfit. Somehow it's managed to make even her skinny legs look fat.

"Chubby Chic?" I say.

I'm joking, of course, but Ramie, psycho that she is, gets that look in her eye.

"No way," I say.

She nods slowly. "Yes, Jill. Yes." She grabs both of my shoulders and looks down on me from her extra six inches. "Chubby Chic. That's perfect."

"You are *not* wearing that."

"Oh, yes I am."

I try to untie the rainbow ribbon around her waist, but she pushes my hand away.

"I am leaving here today with this outfit," she says. "And I am wearing it to school on Monday."

She will too. She'll walk around all day looking like a pink Michelin Man and try to spread the rumor that Chubby Chic is the new black. Weirdest part? Within the week, she'll have a few imitators.

"Hey, you know," she says, "maybe you should pull a Steven Price on Tommy Knutson."

"What do you mean?"

"I mean, make your own preemptive strike."

"You mean, ask Tommy Knutson to the prom?"

"Why not?"

I sit on the edge of the bed. "I never thought of that. It wouldn't be too forward, would it?"

"Guys love it. Take the lead. Why should you wait around for him?"

For Ramie to claim any expertise on what guys love is a bit of a stretch. She's not exactly a hot property at Winterhead High. Don't get me wrong. There isn't a guy at the school who wouldn't *do* Ramie. But I can't think of a single one who would *date* her. As Mom never tires of reminding me, I'd be much more popular if I "reconsidered my loyalty to that girl." But I'm not about being popular. To be honest, the fact that I'm able to live any semblance of a normal teenage life is a surprising bonus, given my potential for catastrophic humiliation. Besides, with Ramie as my BFF, no one can honestly accuse me of being anything but comparatively ordinary.

There is a knock on the door, and Mom breezes right in.

"Hey, Mom," I say. "How's the spying?"

Mom hovers in the doorway. "I was going to heat up some soup for lunch, sweetie. Will Ramie be joining us?" She does not look at Ramie as she says this. Mom once called Ramie a "worshipper of chaos." When I told Ramie, she thought it was cool and threatened to tattoo it on her butt cheek.

"Mom," I say. "We just ate breakfast."

"I know, sweetheart. I want to know how much to defrost." Without making eye contact, she gives Ramie's outfit the up and down. "Jill, is that your dress?"

"It's okay," I say. "I'm deeply over it."

Ramie grabs the stack of magazines from my desk. "I've got to run. I'll let you know what I find out about you-know-who."

"Cool," I say.

Mom's eyes follow Ramie as she flees down the hallway and disappears down the stairs.

"Was that the down vest you absolutely had to have and would die if you didn't get for Christmas?"

"She's not stealing it, Mom. She's just borrowing it."

Mom tugs at the sleeve of her cashmere sweater, then inclines her head at me.

"What?" I say.

"So, you're concerned about the prom?"

"I'm not concerned, Mom. I just want to go with Tommy Knutson."

She narrows her eyes at me.

"What!" I say.

"If he wants to go to the prom with you, sweetie, he'll ask."

"What if he's shy?" I say.

Mom sucks in this gigantic breath, like I've asked her to explain something deeply obvious. Then she pulls out a paperback, which I've just noticed tucked under her arm, and hands it to me.

"The Guide?" I say.

Mom nods. "We didn't have this book when I was your age. We had to improvise."

The subtitle is *Timeless Tips for Landing Mr. Right.* I have a quick flip through it.

"Men are different," Mom says. "The sooner you learn that, the better."

"I don't care about men, Mom. I'm focusing on one man. Tommy Knutson. The rest of them can spontaneously combust as far as I'm concerned."

I put the book on my desk and start picking up the rejected clothes Ramie has flung about my room, including her own, which she's left in a pile.

Mom crosses her arms and leans against the doorjamb. "I know it's hard to believe," she says, "but even at the ripe old age of seventeen, you may not know everything there is to know."

"All right," I say. "I'll read it."

She fires one last condescending glare at me, then leaves. On the one hand, I'm not inclined to take Mom's advice on men. It's not like her marriage to Dad is anything to brag about. They've barely spoken since Dad assumed sole occupancy of our basement. On the other hand, if her stories are to be believed, by the time she graduated from college in Ye Olde Early Eighties, Mom was dripping with "prospects." No less than six guys proposed to her. Six guys!

And she chose Dad. That's the bewildering part. But then, he used to be normal. He used to be a corporate lawyer until he ditched his career on "the eve of partnership, for God's sake," to use Mom's oft-repeated phrase. Mom worked two jobs to put him through law school, so she has an understandably bad attitude about that particular decision. As you've undoubtedly guessed by now, my parents are annoyingly complicated. I try not to think about it.

So anyway, I go to my desk and glance at the first tip, which is "become a being like no other." I'm fairly certain I already *am* a being like no other, but the authors have something else in mind. To them, becoming a being like no other means sipping rather than slurping your drink, pausing between sentences, and—I am not kidding here—"if your hair falls into your face, comb it back from the top of your head in a single graceful sweep."

I turn to my left and practice the move in the mirror above my dresser. It looks deeply fake at first, but when I practice it a few times, it starts to look natural, and I have to admit, there's something surprisingly elegant about it. It beats sticking your hair behind your ears or, worse, wearing a barrette.

I keep reading. Most of the tips involve variations on the theme of playing hard to get. Things like ending a conversation quickly and never calling a guy on the phone. I can't help wondering, though: if everyone who reads this book follows its advice, won't we become beings *just like* every other?

I close the book and look up at my calendar. I now have one hundred and twenty-six days to get Tommy Knutson to ask me to the prom. That may sound like a long time to you, but I don't even have a strategy yet. I pick up Mom's book again. It's a place to start, right?

march 14

Jack

Let me tell you something about Jill. The girl's life is a friggin' fairy tale. I swear she wakes up to the sound of woodland creatures whistling a happy tune at her window. Oh, but it's not all sunshine and roses, right? "Boo friggin' hoo, Steven Price asked me to the prom when I really really really want to go with Tommy Knutsack."

Well, listen up, Little Jilly Wets-her-pants, when your biggest problem is conning some lazy-eyed schmuckwit into asking you to the prom, you can excuse the rest of us for withholding our sobs. Some of us have *real* problems to contend with.

All right, Jack, chill out. Take a few deep breaths.

Sorry. I don't mean to rant. I'm in a bad mood. I'm always in a bad mood when I wake up. It's hormonal. Jill, the lucky bitch, gets three full weeks per cycle to live her stupid life. I get four days. Four *premenstrual* days. How many dudes have that complaint?

But don't go spilling any tears for me. I've got this under control. Jill may have her Plan B rituals. Well, I have Plan Jack rituals. They go like this:

Wake up, check that I'm all in one piece, if you know what I mean, then haul my naked ass out of bed. Jill's been decent enough to sleep naked at the end of her phase ever since I informed her what it felt like to wake up with my nuts twisted into a thong strap. Yes, I have to tell Jill these things. I have to leave her little notes because of all that Plan B stuff she does to obliterate me. I'm telling you, the girl knows *nothing* about my life.

Which means she doesn't know how much *I* know about hers.

So anyway, first thing I do after taking a monster piss in our private bathroom is check the calendar on which Little Anal Annie has dutifully crossed out all the days that have passed. Then I lie right back down to begin my own form of meditation.

Of course, I skip the "I am all girl" crap. I go right to the black dot. It's always there, right in the middle of my forehead where Jill left it. But instead of using it to erase things, I do the opposite. I envision myself squeezing through it like a snake into a rabbit hole. Then I project Jill's last three weeks onto the blackness like a superfast movie and take detailed mental notes of the good parts. I'm not sure she'd appreciate the gory detail in which I record the things she does, says, thinks, lies about, smells, touches and dreams. Would you?

Don't be judgmental, though. Jill's life—that petty, grade-grubbing, Ramie-worshipping life—constitutes my only experience of the outside world. I can't afford to forget things.

That's how it has to be. I'm a realist. I understand the ways of the world. I have no interest in parading our "condition" around like a circus act. Besides, as long as Plan B keeps working, I don't have to worry about them finding a cure. Oh, don't be naive. They'd snuff me like a rabid dog if they could. They tried to. That was Plan A.

Honestly, the fact that "Mom" (and, believe me, I use the term loosely) never came after me with a scalpel is a small miracle. That woman is nuts. You should have seen her reaction on the day I finally woke up. No, not the day Gail Girliepants grew a dick. I'm talking about the day the dick developed an autonomous sense of self. Don't ask me how this transpired. I'm not a shrink. All I know is that in May of our sophomore year, almost a year after the cycling had begun, I stopped feeling like Jill with a penis and started feeling like me.

That was a messed-up day. At dinner I told Mom and Dad I wanted to be called Jack, not Jill, because, you know, I was a guy. You should have seen the look on Mom's face. She jammed her fork into her mashed potatoes and said no way. I should just knock that off right now. The fact that I was suddenly, you know, *alive,* meant nothing to her. In her eyes, I was nothing more than an ugly wart on a pretty girl's cheek. She and Dad talked about locking the bedroom door, even handcuffs. What if I escaped? What if I roamed the neighborhood like the bogeyman? What if I ruined their precious Plan B?

Mom and Dad eventually came to their senses. Well, Mom did. Dad's senses have been MIA for three years now. She decided against handcuffs and door locks and settled for a sturdy parental filter on the Internet. Big miscalculation. I hacked through it in two days, set up a MySpace page and started downloading epic amounts of porn. It was a short-lived victory, though. When Mom found out—who knows how—she canceled the Internet altogether. The next day, she canceled the phone service. Now only she and Jill have cell phones and Mom keeps both of them with her lest I get my dirty hands on one and make pornographic prank calls. Which I would. Believe me.

Mom and I formed a tense truce after that. I stopped trying to leak my hideous self into the outside world. She bought me books, CDs and Nintendo. But things were never the same. I wasn't her child anymore. I was an unwanted houseguest. A *dangerous* unwanted houseguest. After a while, I started having dinner in my bedroom. She didn't mind. She was glad to be rid of me. Dad was harder to read. He always had this guilty look on his face as if he was about to say something but didn't know how to phrase it. What was I supposed to make of that?

I hardly ever leave my room anymore, except to raid the fridge. Sometimes I bump into Dad in the kitchen, but for the most part, he stays in his basement and I stay in my room. When I need something from the outside world, I leave a note for Jill. She's pretty cool about getting me stuff: books, DVDs, that kind of thing. She's all right, I guess. I just wish she wasn't so boring.

It's an issue for me because, like I said, her life is my only window to the outside world. It'd be nice if the girl would cut me some slack and, I don't know, vandalize something, flip off a teacher or maybe experiment with lesbianism. Something. Instead, I'm forced to live vicariously through the tedious non-adventures of Marjorie Model Citizen.

But what can I do? I try to make the best of it. When life gives you lemons, and all that.

So anyway, on March 14, after taking a piss and noting that only one hundred and one days remain to get Tommy Knut-case to ask us to the prom, I lie down, summon the black dot and squeeze through the rabbit hole of Jill's life. I won't bore you with the complete details. Suffice it to say, it goes something like this:

Saw Ramie in a bra . . . speed-read Mom's *Guide* book . . . broke a fingernail . . . tripped over Tony Camere in front of a bunch of football players . . . got Mrs. Wainwright to raise my A– to an A on my *Red Badge of Courage* paper . . . almost wet myself in calculus when Tommy Knutjob looked at me . . . secretively picked my nose in Spanish class . . . practiced Ramie's alluring over-the-shoulder glance in the mirror.

Riveting stuff, right? Bear with me. There is one theme from Harriet Ho-hum's Adventures in Snoozeland that always gets my juices flowing. I spend extra time remembering those sections. I savor every luscious, forbidden detail. If Jill ever knew about this illicit pleasure of mine, she'd freak out. Heck, it scares *me* sometimes. There's something so taboo about it. But what can I do? I'm a flesh-and-blood guy. Just because no one knows I exist, it doesn't mean I don't have needs. In fact, I'm having a need right now. Time to leave Barbara Boredom a note with a new request.

march 18

Jill

Ninety-seven days until prom night.

I wake up with the transformation cleanly behind me, do my Plan B rituals, and take down the handwritten note Jack has taped to the mirror. "Dear Jill," it reads. "Need more porn."

Ick. But I keep reading. "You don't want my dirty mind wandering where it tends to wander, so do us both a favor and get the warden to bring back the Net. Thanks. Jack."

I thought it was mal sharing my bedroom with a smelly boy. Sharing it with a smelly boy who asks me for porn is an extreme dimension of mal.

There's a knock on the door.

"You up?" Mom says.

I open the door and Mom's in full work mode: she's wearing a beige wool-blend pantsuit with regrettably tapered-leg trousers I still have not been able to talk her out of. Her hair is blown and sprayed into strict stasis. But her face brightens into a big warm smile, which creases the corners of her eyes.

"What day is it?" I say.

"Sunday," she says. "I'm taking Pamela's shift today."

I nod, cross off the four previous days on my calendar.

She ruffles my hair and says, "French toast?"

I nod.

When she's gone, I shower, throw on some jeans and a T-shirt, then head downstairs.

Normally, Dad eats breakfast in his basement yoga hole, but the smell of maple syrup warming on the stove always brings him up. He lurks in the doorway between the kitchen and the living room. "Hey, pumpkin," he says.

"That's an unusually festive ensemble," I say.

Dad's fashion sense is disgusting on his best days, but today he's wearing heavy green slipper socks, turquoise swimming trunks with a giant bleach stain on the right leg and a holey Three Stooges T-shirt somebody gave him for his birthday a thousand years ago.

"Wait a minute," I say. "Dad, have you been scavenging the Goodwill bag?"

He curtsies and says, "Waste not, want not."

Believe it or not, this passes for joviality in the McTeague household.

Dad and I pull out our chairs and have a seat under the fluorescent glare of the breakfast nook while Mom pours the syrup into the little Pilgrim gravy boat and joins us.

"You feeling okay this morning?" he asks.

"Aces," I tell him. I spear two slices of French toast and drag them to my plate.

There's frost on the little window over the steel kitchen sink, and the trees in the background are gray and bare. A typical crappy day in Winterhead. But inside, things are nice and cozy, with Dad's ever-present oniony aroma creating an unusual counterpoint to the homey smell of hot butter and maple syrup.

"So," I say. "Jack wants you guys to bring back the Internet."

Dad drops his fork with a clatter and Mom freezes with the gravy boat mid-pour. They hate when I bring up Jack.

"Why?" Mom blinks about a thousand times as she says this.

I'm a fairly creative person, but it is way too early to make something up, so I just come out with it. "He wants porn. He said if he doesn't get it, his mind will wander somewhere I don't want it to. Don't ask me what that means. I don't want to know." I pour myself some OJ.

Dad starts tugging on his beard, then jabs his fork into the platter of French toast and drags a piece back to his plate.

I look at Mom, whose face has reverted to its normal state of robotic calm.

"Loan him your father's," she says. "He's got a stack of old *Hustlers* hidden in a box downstairs. Next to his hockey equipment."

I do not look at my dad. I think I will never look at my dad again. But through my peripheral vision, I can see his knuckles whitening around his fork.

Mom chews her tiny mouthful while smiling that robot smile, as if this were all perfectly normal. Then she pours herself another cup of coffee. "Don't worry about it, sweetheart."

She empties half a packet of Sweet'n Low into her Relax, There's a Woman on the Job mug. "All boys do it." She stirs her coffee and takes a dainty sip. "They're only a baby step above chimps."

Dad's white knuckles release the fork, letting it drop again to the plate.

Mom slices off a corner of her French toast, pops it in her mouth and winks at me.

"Mom," I say. "I am not giving him Dad's . . . magazines." I can't even say the words "porn" and "Dad" in the same sentence.

"Well, I'm not bringing the Internet back into this house," Mom says. "Not after last time."

"I think Jack learned his lesson after that," I say. "He's been good, right?"

Mom levels a cold gaze at me like I'm being naive, but sometimes I think she enjoys assuming the worst about Jack. About all men, actually.

"Well, what should we do?" I say. "Jack says he needs it."

Mom gives Dad a wide-eyed look like she's expecting him to come up with an idea, but Dad hasn't come up with an idea in years. Dad is an idea-free zone. I lower my head and sneak a sideways glance at him. He keeps his eyes on his plate while he stabs a piece of French toast and makes it bleed syrup. When he glances up at Mom, waves of silent hatred propagate between their eyes. Mom's smile never wavers. She can propagate hate waves while smiling, doing her nails, cooking dinner, you name it.

After a few seconds of frigid standoff, Mom lays her fork and knife across her plate. "Fine," she says. "I'll pick up some magazines after work. Okay?" Though she looks at me while she says this, it's clearly directed at Dad for being basically a nonentity in this household.

"Thanks, Mom," I tell her.

She waves her hand dismissively, then knocks back the rest of her coffee. "I've got to get to the office." She takes her plate to the sink, dumps the remains in the rubbish, gives it a quick rinse and puts it in the dishwasher—all without a single wasted motion. Then she breezes out of the kitchen as if we have not just discussed pornography over French toast.

That leaves me and Dad.

The phone rings and I leap from the table, vowing to engage in a lengthy chat with whomever is on the other end, even if it's Auntie Billie.

"Hey, Jill."

It's Ramie, bless her.

"Guess what?" she says.

I take the phone out of the kitchen and slump into the beige sofa in the living room. A "guess what" from Ramie could mean anything.

"I got into FIT," she says.

"Nice one!" I say. "Not that I'm surprised, you little genius, you."

FIT is the Fashion Institute of Technology in New York City.

"I wish you were coming with me," she says.

"Tell me about it," I sigh.

I'd give anything to go away to college, but unfortunately, Plan B will not work in a dorm, so I'm stuck with deeply mal . Groton College, which is a Christian college in Winterhead.

"It's not too late," Ramie says. "You could apply for second semester. I could take care of you, drive you to your treatments and stuff. We could be roomies."

Yeah, *that* would work.

I haven't ruled out the possibility of transferring to a commutable school in Boston at some point, but Mom thinks I should stay close to home, at least for the first year.

"Ramie," I say. "I am going to Groton to find Jesus."

"Is he missing?"

Truthfully, college is not something I like to think about. The future, in general, is a big ball of scary. When I imagine what it will be like when I can no longer reasonably live at home, I tend to break out in hives. Not that I want to be one of those losers who never moves out. It's just that Mom and I haven't figured out how to evolve Plan B into Plan C: Independent Living. Mom thinks we should shelve worrying about that for a later date. I'm on board with that.

"Rames," I say. "I'm really happy for you."

"Thanks," she says, but it's dripping with moroseness.

"Well, don't spoil the fun, dude. You're going to FIT and I'll deeply visit you."

"Promise?"

"Duh. So anyway. College schmollege, what have you got for me?"

"Right," she says. "Phase One of the Tommy Knutson Project is complete."

"Shhh. We're not calling it that," I remind her. "It's called Project X."

I can hear Dad's forlorn fork and knife tapping the plate as he finishes his French toast in solitude.

"Well, I've got video," Ramie says. "Want to come over and practice?"

"First things first," I say. "What have you learned about our prime target?"

"He's not a drug dealer," she says.

"Excellent."

"Thought you'd like that," she says. "Additionally, he was never a prostitute on Hollywood Boulevard."

"What?" I almost fall off the sofa. "I never heard that one."

"Yeah," she says. "The guy comes with a complete set of false rumors. I'm skimming this data from a sea of gossip and innuendo."

"But you're sure they're false?"

"Absolutely," she says. "I got most of my reliable intel from some kids in his art class who say they don't talk to him much anymore."

"Why not?" I say.

"Unknown," she says. "They got all shruggy and evasive when I asked. I have to say, Jill, the guy does have a quasi-mysterious loner-type vibe."

"Is that bad?"

"Could go either way."

"You mean, maybe he's so superior to his fellow students," I say, "that he has no need of their deeply inferior companionship?"

"Or," she says, "he's on the verge of shooting up the school. Yeah, that's what I mean."

I hear myself swallow. But I deeply do not think Tommy Knutson is *that* type of loner. His eyes are too kind.

"Oh," Ramie says, "and apparently, he had some sort of devastating relationship in New York with an older girl named Tinsley."

"Tinsley?"

"It's a rich girl's name," she says, "which is good news, given what we're about to turn you into."

"Good point."

I hear Dad screech his chair and take his plate to the dishwasher.

"So, you want to come over and practice?" Ramie says.

"There in fifteen." I hang up and return the phone to its cradle in the kitchen.

"Gotta run," I tell Dad.

I do not look at him when I say it. By now, I'm pretty much committed to never looking at him again.

Now, I'm going to go out on a limb here and say that Project X (a.k.a. the Tommy Knutson Project) is the second-greatest achievement of the McTeague household (with Plan B holding steady in the number one spot). Ramie and I fine-tuned Project X before Jack's phase while holed up in my bedroom for a nacho-fueled all-nighter. Mom thought we were cramming for a Spanish test. At least she pretended to think that. She approves of neither Ramie's existence nor my obsession with Tommy Knutson but has, for some reason, chosen to back off. Most likely, she has me under twenty-four-hour surveillance and is pretending to butt out because Project X centers around her *Guide* book. You see, we have turned Mom's book into an action plan. How? By transforming me into a being like no other. According to *The Guide,* this is supposed to trigger the hunter instinct in men, thus compelling them to propose marriage or, in my case, a date to the prom. And since "being like no other" is a euphemism for "aloof, unattainable snob," Ramie and I have decided to use as our role model Alexis Oswell, a.k.a. Lexie, the Rich Bitch.

Lexie is, by a wide margin, the aloofest and unattainablest girl at Winterhead High. All her friends go to private school, but her gazillionaire parents make her go to public school because they have political opinions on the subject. Lexie has never voluntarily spoken to anyone at Winterhead High. Nevertheless, she's made the guys' Top Five Most Doable list four years running. So has Ramie. I got honorable mention once, along with twenty other girls.

So, while I was away getting my "blood transfusions," Ramie got sneaky with her cell phone camera and recorded Lexie strutting through the hallways of Winterhead High. I suppose I should point out that Ramie does not approve of *The Guide*. It's "archaic" and "objectifying" and "antifeminist" and a whole host of other things she assures me I will care about when I achieve her exalted state of enlightenment. She's only participating in the Tommy Knutson Project—I mean, Project X—because it's an opportunity to attempt "rebranding," which is a concept she read about in British *Vogue*. She said that turning me into Lexie Oswell is like turning the Gap into Chanel. Then she apologized and bought me some expensive mint tea because I am *not* the Gap.

When I get to Ramie's house, she ushers me right upstairs.

"What happened to Chubby Chic?" I ask her. "You're wearing skinny jeans again."

She sits me down on her ancient lumpy brass bed and grabs her laptop, where she's downloaded the Alexis Oswell footage. "Yeah," she says, "I've had a rethink of Chubby Chic." She sits cross-legged next to me on the thick down comforter and clicks her video software. "Turns out Chubby Chic is not as paradigm shifting as I thought, given the overall lardassification of the American public."

"Lardassification?"

She adjusts the screen brightness. "Yeah. My new word of the week. What do you think?"

I sit cross-legged on the bed. "It's nice, Rames. Sensitive, you know, to fat people."

"Right," she says. "Good point. Anyway, here is the lovely and talented Alexis Oswell." She clicks Play with a flourish, and Lexie's grainy butt and legs begin moving in and out of focus through the crowded hallway near the art room at

Winterhead High. "It's a little jerky," Ramie says. "A cinematographer I am not."

We examine Lexie's walk from a variety of angles and determine that there are exactly four main elements to her overall presentation:

1. Shoulders erect
2. Head tilted back
3. Eyes focused on the distance
4. Hips utterly stationary

That last element is the biggest challenge. I'm sort of bowlegged and my hips tend to sway of their own accord. To achieve Lexie's snooty, stick-up-the-butt walk, Ramie has to grab on to both of my hips and hold them steady while I shuffle back and forth in front of her bed.

"Stop swaying!" she says.

But my hips won't obey.

She lets go and says, "Watch me."

She stands by the ancient hissing radiator under the frosty window and tries the walk herself.

"Ramie," I say. "You walk like a trucker."

She stops in front of the antique beveled mirror above her white dresser, backs up and clomps toward it again. "Mal," she says. "You're right. I never realized how unfeminine I am."

"Yeah, well, your boobs make up for it. Anyway, let's focus on me here."

After several tries, I manage to tame my wayward hips by

clenching my buttocks and forcing my feet to point outward like a duck.

Ramie sprawls on the bed with the laptop at eye level and checks my walk against the Lexie footage.

"No, no, no," she says. "You look like Frankenstein. Your upper body is too stiff."

I stop at her window and shake out my legs and arms. "I think I'm cramping up. Do I at least have the bottom half down?"

"Do it again!" she says.

I take a deep breath, clench my buttocks and duckwalk the three strides to her dresser, watching my reflection the whole way.

"Actually," she says, "that's not bad. You look constipated, but if you loosen up your shoulders and relax your face, it won't be so mal."

Mastering the upper body is much easier and comes with the discovery that "looking down your nose at people" is not a metaphor but an actual posture. With her cell phone, Ramie videos me walking a few short laps; then I join her on the bed and we compare it to the Lexie footage.

"Pretty good," she says. "I feel myself hating you."

"Yes," I say. "But you respect me, don't you? I intrigue."

Ramie raises an eyebrow.

"What?" I say.

"Nothing." She closes the laptop and sits up.

I sit up too. "Ramie!"

She sighs. "You're not exactly approachable like this."

"Do you have Alzheimer's?" I say. "That's the whole point. It's not about being approachable. It's about becoming a 'high-status' woman."

"Right," she says. But there's doubt in her eyes.

"Ramie," I say. "I need you on board with this. If you have concerns, I need to know them now."

"Nope," she says. "I'm on board. You become an uptight snob. Tommy is bound to want you."

"*Aloof,* not uptight."

"Right. You become an aloof snob, while I dig for signs that Tommy is growing wild with desire to hunt you."

I drop my head into my hands.

"Well, I'm sorry," she says. "But you have to admit this is a pretty non-sane philosophy."

"Who cares?" I tell her. "As long as it works." I pull myself off the bed and walk over to her assortment of vintage trench coats hung from a row of wooden hooks. Above them is a framed photo of Greta Garbo smoking a cigarette and looking all classy. Talk about a high-status woman.

"Look," I tell her. "I've tried it the other way, being friendly, being approachable. It's not getting me a date with Tommy Knutson, is it? Boys are different."

"You sound like your mother."

"Shut up," I say. "It's just a fact, Ramie. It's science. If we want them to act on their natural male instincts as hunters, we have to play our part as—"

"Gatherers?" she says.

"No!" I say. "As prey." I grab the belt from one of the trench coats and start fiddling with it. "I thought you were on board with this. You got the Lexie footage."

Ramie cocks her head as she sizes me up.

"What?" I say.

"This isn't just about getting a prom date, is it?"

"What do you mean?"

"You heart him."

"I do not." I look down and start winding the belt around my finger. "He's just a decent prom prospect, you know, being new and kind of a loner."

"Jill," she says, "if it were only about getting a prom date, you could have said yes to Steven Price."

"Are you psychoanalyzing me?"

Ramie nods.

I wrap the belt around my finger even tighter.

"Look at you," she says. "You're in a severe state of Tommy positiveness. You're Tommified. You're a Knutsonian."

"Are you finished?"

"Your finger's purple."

"Ow." I unwrap the belt and shake out my hand. "All right," I say. "Maybe I kind of, sort of heart him a little bit."

"I knew it!" she says. "Well, this changes everything."

"Why?"

"Because!" she says. "It's not a lame prom strategy anymore. It's a bona fide slurpy love thing." Ramie smiles giddily and hugs her pillow. "It's so cool."

"It is not," I say. "I have to act like he doesn't exist, Ramie. Like he's a black hole."

"A deeply peculiar dilemma," she says.

"Ramie, you can't bail out on me. Not now."

"I'm not going anywhere," she says. With renewed vigor, she picks up the cell phone and points it at me. "All right, let's do this thing."

I back up to Ramie's radiator, straighten my shoulders, tilt my head back and walk the Lexie walk.

Curse my stupid heart. It was only supposed to be about the prom.

Monday, March 19. Ninety-six days until prom night. Look out, Winterhead High. The new and improved, ingeniously rebranded Jill McTeague has arrived. Butt clenched, shoulders erect, I glide through the teeming hallways. Nose scornfully aloft, I make eye contact with no one. In fact, my gaze is so focused on the distance that I overshoot my homeroom door and Ramie has to drag me inside by the belt loop.

But by the time D Block Spanish rolls around, I am in command of the Lexie Oswell walk and am starting to feel the mojo of this new attitude. Mercifully, Tommy is absent, which means I have the whole day to practice my new persona.

To aid in the transformation, I have taken a page from Plan B and composed a new mantra: "I am a busy girl with a rich, full life. I am confident, strong and beautiful, and any man would be lucky to have me." I repeat this silently to myself as I glide through the drab gray hallways of Winterhead High, where my graceless peers scurry to and fro. I am above them all. I am just out of reach. I am . . .

A being.

Like.

No other.

I'm so good at this act, I forget to turn it off when I meet Ramie for lunch and she has to whack me on the shoulder and say, "Snap out of it, bitch."

You do not condescend to Ramie Boulieaux.

Day One of Project X swims along, well, swimmingly. But on Day Two, Tommy finally appears. It's just after homeroom, and I'm heading to history class when I spot his pale chiseled face and brown shoulder-length hair in the distance behind a cluster of giggling freshgirls. His white button-down shirt is loose and open just one button at the collar, revealing, even from three classrooms away, the tender notch at his collarbone. I've never gotten close enough to smell Tommy Knutson, but I'm sure he smells like heaven. Angels do, you know. And the way he moves. He's like a stingray—graceful and smooth amid the chaotic frenzy of dizzy fish all around him. He, not I, is the being like no other.

And I'm staring at him! I take a deep breath, close my locker and pull my pale blue cashmere sweater down over the waistband of my black jeans. Eyes on the distance, head tilted back, I shoulder my backpack and head toward him. My pulse races as I sense him getting closer to me. I clench my butt cheeks and focus more intently on the art room at the end of the hallway. But just ahead and to the right of me are Jed Barnsworthy and his cluster of toady boys loitering, per usual, by the special needs room for another round of teasing the developmentally disabled kids. Jed lives two houses down from me, but I don't speak to him anymore unless absolutely necessary. Now, though, in a freak confluence of events, Tommy approaches me just as I approach Jed, and for a brief but tragic moment, we are all drawn into a hideous Jed Barnsworthy vortex.

"Hey, McTeague," Jed says. "What's with the stupid walk? Something lodged up your ass? Need me to dig it out?" He laughs like a hyena.

My heart races, but I keep my pace constant, eyes front. Through peripheral vision, I see Tommy Knutson stop and face Jed. Then I hear laughter. Snarling, toady-boy laughter. Plus laughter from other sources I'm too shaken to identify. Stifling the urge to run, I continue gliding away, past the trophy case toward the art room.

Does Tommy say something to Jed? Does he notice my unshaken calm in the face of social disgrace? I will never know. I duckwalk down the hall until there is nowhere to go but into the art room, despite the fact that I need to be in history class, which is on the other side of the school. The sophomore students gathering their India ink and styluses look at me in confusion, but I don't care. I can't risk having Tommy Knutson spot me peering out of the classroom like a scared mouse. I am above all this, you see. I am a high-status woman, and this kind of juvenile nonsense does not concern me.

I wait for the late bell, then hightail it out of the art room. At the special needs room, which wormy Jed Barnsworthy has mercifully vacated, I turn right down the North Wing, skidding on my gold flats. Dodging other stragglers, I slip into history class just as Mr. Bennett is about to close the door.

"Thanks for joining us, Jill," he says.

Do I respond? No. I take my seat and make eye contact with no one. Project X requires one hundred percent commitment. It is not for dabblers.

By the end of Week One, evidence of Project X's success begins to trickle in. Lindsay Siggersall and her cheerleader pals are spotted mocking my new walk in the cafeteria to thunderous laughter from nearby tables. Daria Benedetti, my Spanish study buddy, pulls me aside after class to ask if I'm mad at her. At first I feign ignorance so as to keep up the act, because Daria has very loose lips. But it's too hard to lie to a friend, so instead, I apologize profusely and explain Project X. She understands, having spent her entire sophomore year pining for senior basketball star Lawrence Fogerty, who wound up impregnating an Esswich girl and skipping town a week before graduation.

By the middle of Week Two, the evidence is overwhelming. I have replaced Alexis Oswell as the coldest girl at Winterhead High. There are even rumors that my new attitude has something to do with my "mysterious absences." The words "brain tumor" are bandied about. But the full price of Project X doesn't become clear to me until one day in chem lab.

Steven Price and I are heating a saline solution over our shared Bunsen burner when he starts swallowing compulsively, which is a nervous tic. I know from Wikipedia that you're not supposed to draw attention to someone's nervous tic, so I sigh happily and say, "So, how are things, Steven?"

He shoots me a frightened look, then scowls and returns his gaze to the Bunsen burner.

"Steven," I say. "Look, I'm sorry if I've been—"

"It's okay," he says. "No biggie."

He makes a big show of concentrating on the solution bubbling in the beaker.

"Steven, listen. There's a reason I've been . . ."

He looks up and waits for me to finish. But I never do. Steven undoubtedly thinks my new frigidity is the result of his preemptive prom attack. I want to dissuade him, but I can't tell him about Project X. He'll think I'm ridiculous. Plus he'll never forgive me for choosing Tommy Knutson over him.

"Nothing," I say.

He looks down again and swallows three times in a row. For a short but desperate moment, I want to abandon Project X or at least make an exception for Steven. I want to throw my arms around him, hug all his nervous tics away and tell him how special and wonderful he is.

But that is not what a *Guide* girl does.

Instead, I stare at the bubbles in our beaker, then look up at the clock and pray for a fire drill to slice off the remaining twenty-two minutes of chem lab.

Like I said. *One hundred percent commitment.* Not for dabblers.

I have alienated everyone: friends, acquaintances, even a few teachers, who, it seems, are not above maligning me in the faculty lounge within earshot of chatty students. Project X is a success.

But (and yes, it's a big one) Ramie has gleaned no news

about Tommy Knutson. If my new status as aloof snob—I mean, a being like no other—is, in fact, driving him wild with desire to hunt me down like prey, the lad is keeping it to himself. He has asked no one why I don't look at him in H Block calculus anymore. He has indicated to no one that he has noticed a change in my behavior. And, more critically, he has said nary a peep on the subject of the prom, which is beginning to loom like a storm cloud full of lightning. The boy is, to use Ramie's term, "a total data abyss."

So one day, I enter the cafeteria, doing my snooty walk, and approach Ramie and Daria, the only people I am permitted to speak with.

"My butt is killing me," I say.

Daria makes room for me and I sit next to her.

"Yeah," she says. "And everyone's starting to hate you."

"Really?"

Ramie pulls out her cell phone. "I can confirm new artwork in the North Wing boys' room." She shows me the picture—a graffiti drawing of a stick figure with what looks like a firecracker exploding from its butt. Underneath it is written "Her Royal Highness, Jill McTeague."

"That's good news?" I say.

Ramie snaps her cell phone shut. "They didn't do it when you were nice."

I take out my own cell phone, look at the date and do a quick calculation. "Eighty-seven days till zero hour," I say. "I don't know how much longer I can keep this up."

Ramie sips from a bottle of Italian soda. "The thing is," she says, "with this *Guide* business? It's more of a filtering system than an attainment strategy."

I take out my peanut butter and jelly sandwich. "Expand."

"I mean, it's fine if you can wait all your life for a guy who's so obsessed he'll hunt your snobby ass down and propose marriage, but—"

"It's not proactive, is it?" I say.

Daria steals a potato chip from me. "Yeah, well, the whole *Guide* philosophy is a lesson in enforced passivity."

I glare at Ramie, because that was deeply not a Daria thought.

"What?" Ramie says. "You have to admit she has a point. I mean, how's Tommy supposed to give you what you want if he has no idea what that is? Bit of a problem, no?"

"No," I say. "The problem is one of focus."

Ramie and Daria exchange doubtful looks. Obviously, they have been bad-mouthing Project X behind my back, the dirty traitors.

"Think about it," I say. "I'm broadcasting my high status to everyone. But that's like putting up a billboard and just hoping the right customer drives by. I should be aiming my high status directly at Tommy Knutson."

"Like a weapon," Ramie says.

"Exactly."

"But how?" Daria says.

Ramie inhales sharply as if a lightbulb has just gone off. "By getting him alone," she says.

"Without violating *The Guide*," I clarify.

Daria sucks her teeth. "Deeply challenging."

"Deeply, deeply," Ramie says. "But not impossible. Jill, what are your thoughts on skiing?"

"Apathetic to hostile," I say. "Rames, you know I don't ski."

"Reconsider that," she says.

Thus was born Operation Swoon.

Winterhead is practically in the Arctic. We have our own ski slope. It's not the Alps or anything, just a smallish hill anchored by a wooden shack that rents skis and serves hot cocoa. We call it the Bump. But did I spend every single wintry day of my childhood going up and down this glorified snowdrift? No. I took cooking classes inside, where it was warm. Damn my lack of foresight.

So guess who loves skiing with a passion that, in Ramie's snooped lingo, "approaches religion"? You guessed it. Tommy Knutson. And guess where Tommy Knutson spends his weekends?

The Bump.

All day Saturday. All day Sunday. He even teaches beginner skiing to little kids on Wednesday afternoons. How adorable is that?

For a smaller mind, this not-inconsiderable deviation in our respective interests might signal a stumbling block to prom-related coupling. Not for the talented trio of Jill McTeague, Ramie Boulieaux and Daria Benedetti.

Here's the plan.

Daria will wait in my Nissan in the Bump parking lot, on the lookout for Tommy Knutson's silver Prius, which, according to

Ramie's sources, always arrives between nine-thirty and eleven-thirty every Saturday and every Sunday. As soon as she spots it, she'll call my cell phone and Ramie and I will take up first positions. Ramie will be stationed inside the cocoa shack. I'll be outside by the ski racks. When Tommy comes out to put his skis on, I'll toss him a big warm smile and wave. I know. I know. Not a *Guide* move at all. Be patient.

Now, Tommy, who has never been on the receiving end of so brash and unfeminine a gesture from me, will be confused. *Is she waving at me?* he'll wonder. *Wow! What a gorgeous smile.* Etc., etc. Then, being a gentleman, he'll wave shyly in return.

Here's where it gets interesting. I'll sigh exasperatedly and wave an even bigger wave, then crank up the smile into a full-blown laugh. (I've practiced this transition with Ramie and her cell phone camera. I'm not Julia Roberts or anything, but so long as I don't squint, I can achieve something in the vicinity of Julia brilliance.) This is meant to confuse Tommy. *What's she laughing at?* he'll wonder. *Is my fly down? Am I emboogered?* Out of politeness, he'll wave back and laugh nervously along with me.

That's when we turn the screws on him.

Using my finely manicured right pointer finger, I'll beckon him toward me while shaking my head as if he were a very naughty boy. (I've practiced this look extensively so as to avoid the allure-killing scowl.) Tommy, bewildered now by this totally unprecedented breach of the common laws of aloof femininity, will glance behind him to make sure that I am not, in fact, beckoning someone else. Then, being a gentleman and not incurious as to my intentions, he'll walk somewhat hesitantly toward me.

When he is halfway there, we'll unleash the Grand Twist.

Ramie, all flustered, will run out of the cocoa shack, cell phone in hand, and plunk herself right between Tommy and me. "So sorry, darling," she'll say. Air kiss. Air kiss. "I wasn't ignoring you. I was on the phone with the fashion editor from Paris *Vogue*." (Ramie insisted on that part.)

Now picture the tableau: Ramie and I united at last and Tommy Knutson feeling utterly foolish for thinking that I was so brazen a girl as to beckon him to me. But lest you think the plan ends here, there is one final turn of the screw.

Ramie and I will walk away, leaving an embarrassed Tommy Knutson behind. Then Ramie, klutz that she is, will drop a ski glove and turn to retrieve it. What do I do? Oh, only unleash the alluring over-the-shoulder glance. Head downward, gaze upward to enlarge the eyes and evoke a sense of innocent vulnerability, I'll look not *at* Tommy Knutson, but just past him. Poor Tommy, overcome now with a love he can barely comprehend for this being like no other, will simply collapse in the snow.

That, ladies and gentlemen, is Operation Swoon.

It takes the passive approach of Mom's *Guide* book and sharpens it into a deadly weapon, all the while preserving the underlying principle of hunter and prey that makes femininity so powerful and mysterious a force.

So Saturday morning rolls around. It's ten-fifteen and Ramie and I have downed three cups of cocoa in the insufficiently heated cocoa shack while Daria waits in my Nissan for Tommy

Knutson to make his promised arrival. I'm swanked out in Ramie's pale pink ski suit with green figure-flattering stripes. My hair is blown perfectly straight and my makeup is light and natural. I've got lip gloss, blush and eyeliner stashed in the pockets of my coat for touch-ups. Ramie, sporting last year's blue ski suit, stares longingly through the steamy little window at the dozen or so skiers going up the rope tow and down the slope.

At 10:47, she turns from the window and says, "I just timed Sarah Mecklenburg. I swear, we can get up and down in under three minutes. That's plenty of time to get into first positions."

From the hard wooden bench where I've sat anxiously for going on two hours, I remind Ramie that I do not ski.

"It's barely an incline, Jill," she says. "Little kids make the run on their very first lesson." She reaches into her tight back pocket and pulls out a wad of twenties.

"What are you doing?" I say.

She walks over to Norm, the ski rental and day pass guy, who sits in a little closet in front of an army of upright skis. "Two day passes, please," she says.

Norm glances up from his car magazine and looks at me questioningly.

"I'm not skiing," I tell him.

"She's just nervous," Ramie says. "Two day passes, please."

Norm palms the twenty. "It's your money," he says. Then he hands Ramie two day passes.

Ramie peels her day pass from its backing and sticks it to

her jacket. "I can't believe you've never even tried it, Jill. You should deeply come to Sugarloaf with us."

She tries to hand me the day pass, but I pivot away and face the smelly popcorn machine. "Why would I want to go to Sugarloaf, Ramie? Why would I want to spend *more* time outside?"

"Because winter is so much more fun if you ski."

"Winter is for suckers." I cross my arms over my chest.

Undaunted, Ramie peels my day pass from its backing and slaps it over my left boob.

"Ouch."

"There," she says. "Now you have to ski."

"Gee, Rames, I guess you got me there. It's not like I can just sit here and ignore the sticker."

"Exactly." She grabs my arm and tries to drag me off the bench.

I hold firm with my other hand. "Get off me, you psycho."

Ramie lets go and stamps her foot on the wooden floor. "I can't believe you want to just sit here and wait for—"

I leap up and slap my hand over Ramie's big fat mouth. "Ramie, we promised 'Melissa' we'd be waiting in the cocoa shack when she got here. Remember?"

She tears my hand from her face and squeezes it hard. "I'm sure 'Melissa' will understand if we take one eensy weensy run on the Bump. After all, we must look like a couple of idiots sitting here waiting for 'Melissa' when we could be skiing." She flicks her eyes to Norm.

Norm is staring at us, mouth opened, but only vaguely intrigued.

As much as I hate to admit it, Ramie's right. Norm must know Tommy. It'll be suspicious indeed if we sit around in the cocoa shack until Tommy arrives.

"Fine," I say. "One time."

Ramie bounces in glee, then goes to Norm and rents me a pair of skis.

Let the record show that it was under the influence of too much cocoa that I made what will undoubtedly stand as one of my top five worst decisions.

The rope tow is out of the question. I am simply not grabbing on to that high-speed rope-burn machine to get dragged uphill at a million miles an hour with a pair of chopsticks bolted to my feet. But so zealous is Ramie to make a skier out of me that she risks her own cred to teach me how to use the much kinder J-bar—basically a hunk of metal shaped, as the name would suggest, into a J and hanging from a very slow-moving rope tow. We have the J-bar to ourselves because, as Ramie explains, "only bed-wetting babies have ever been seen on the J-bar."

Now, the secret to successful J-bar mastery amounts apparently to one golden rule: Don't Sit Down.

"Whatever you do," Ramie says, "just lean against the bar like this."

Ramie demonstrates by positioning herself between two slow-moving and widely spaced J's, then lets one tap her just above the tailbone. She then holds on to the upright part of the

J and lets it carry her slowly up the hill. After a few seconds, she skis away from it and back toward me.

"Easy as pie," she says. "Your turn."

I wait for a J to pass, then slap my big dumb skis into position.

"Keep them straight," she says.

I straighten my skis into a perfect parallel, then look over my shoulder until I feel the J-bar tap me just above the tailbone. Grabbing the upright bar with my right hand, I cling to the horizontal bar with my left.

"Keep your skis straight!" Ramie shouts.

I straighten them out and slowly, very slowly, the J-bar carries me up the hill. To my right, rope-tow jockeys point and snicker at me. Like it's some big accomplishment to hold on to a piece of rope.

"I'll meet you up there!" Ramie shouts.

I don't turn around or acknowledge her because I'm focused on leaning, not sitting, while keeping my skis perfectly, mathematically parallel. Plus I'm gripping both bars of the J as if my life depended on it. Eventually, Ramie passes me on the rope tow and blows me a kiss.

That's when tragedy strikes.

I raise my left hand from the horizontal bar to wave at her when, lo and behold, the bar slips past my tailbone. Gripping it firmly, I try to adjust it back into position but it keeps sliding down the backs of my thighs. Before I know it, I'm toppling backward over the J-bar. My head and shoulders land in the snow. The horizontal bar snags behind my knees, and in the struggle to slide my legs off, my skis crisscross and somehow get stuck together.

Slowly, very slowly, the J-bar hauls me up the hill like a side of beef.

I struggle to jerk my legs off the bar but can generate no traction against the slick snow sliding beneath my back and head. Dropping my ski poles, I grab the bar and try to push it forward beyond my knees, but the moving surface beneath me and the natural wobble of the J-bar prevent any progress. My blush slips out of my coat pocket and slides backward down the hill.

Beaten, I lay back and stare at the stubborn X of my conjoined skis against the blinding white sky. At the top of the hill, an assortment of gears grind each J-bar through a one-hundred-and-eighty-degree turn to send it back down the hill.

My right boob vibrates.

Scrambling out of my ski gloves, I unzip my jacket and dig out my cell phone. My lip gloss tumbles free.

"First positions!" Daria says.

"Oh mal."

"He's . . . hold on," she says. "He's getting out of the car and heading for the cocoa shack. Are you in positions?"

The whish of snow beneath my head and the clang of my conjoined skis against the upright bar almost drown out Daria's voice. Using all my strength, I try to yank my skis apart, but they won't budge. Lifting my butt off the snow in an improvised pelvic thrust, I succeed only in dislodging my eyeliner from the pocket and launching it in a low arc over my head.

"Daria," I say, "listen to me. We have to abort!"

"What? Why?" she says.

"Get to the cocoa shack now!" I tell her.

At the top of the hill, the J-bar lurches violently but fails to slough me off.

"Look!" someone yells.

My J sweeps through the switching gears with a clamorous grinding of metal, then reverses direction to head downhill.

"Where are you?" Daria's tinny voice shouts in my ear. I can hear her getting out of my car and crunching through the gravel parking lot.

As the J heads downhill, it begins to rise off the ground.

"Oh, no," I say.

"What?" Daria says. "What's happening?"

First my back, then my neck, and finally my head are lifted off the ground.

Through the cell phone, I hear the telltale squeak of the cocoa shack door. "Where are you?" Daria whispers.

Dangling now from the backs of my knees, my skis still married in their infernal X, I try not to look at the snowy ground ten feet below. Clumps of wet snow slide from my neck through my upside-down hair.

"Daria," I say. "Listen to me. I don't care what you have to do to make this happen, but you cannot let Tommy Knutson out of the cocoa shack! Do you understand?"

"I'm in the cocoa shack now," she whispers. "Where are you?"

As the J-bar carries me downhill, Ramie skis past me with an astonished look on her face.

"He's talking to that Norm guy," Daria says. "What do I do?"

"Abort!" I say. "Abort mission!"

"How do we abort?"

The J-bar starts to lower toward the ground. That's when I notice that everyone on the Bump has stopped skiing and is pointing in horror at my airborne carcass.

"Jill!" Ramie screams. At the bottom of the hill, she yanks her boots out of her skis and clambers up toward me.

"Get me down!" I yell to her. Into the phone I say, "Daria, are you aborting?"

Ramie shuffles quickly beneath me. "My God," Ramie says. "Are you talking to Daria?" She wraps her arms around my thighs and tries to yank them free. "How on earth did you . . ." She pulls at my left ski, but it won't budge. "Hold on." She jams her fist into the boot mechanism and rips my left foot free. I topple over backward, but impossibly, my right ski catches on the upright bar.

"What the hell!" Ramie says.

The J-bar drags me downhill by the ankle while Ramie, clinging to my right leg, clomps alongside in her ski boots.

"Daria?" I say. "Where are you? Where's Tommy?"

"Oh mal," Daria says.

Jamming her fist into my right boot mechanism, Ramie yanks my boot out of the ski and I tumble free just as the

J-bar heads into the switching gears to reverse itself back up the hill.

I lie in the cold snow and take exactly one relieved breath, then bring my cell phone to my ear. "Daria?"

There is a pause. "Um," she says. "I'm sorry. I didn't know how to abort."

I peel my head up from the snow and stare at the twenty or so people standing in a loose semicircle at my feet.

Among them are Daria and Tommy Knutson.

Tommy steps forward and drops to his knees in the snow beside me. "Are you all right?" he says.

His breath fogs the cold air and smells of peppermint. I don't answer him.

I feel Ramie's hand on my shoulder. "Jill?" she says, dropping to her knees.

Tommy looks at Ramie. "You think she's in shock?"

Ramie shrugs. "Jill," she says. "Are you hurt? Can you hear me?"

Ramie's breath does not smell of peppermint.

Somehow (it's all a bit of a blur) Ramie and Tommy get me up and we trudge past the murmuring crowd in our ski boots. Clumps of wet snow slither between my jacket and sweater.

Once we're in the cocoa shack, Tommy sits me down on one of the wooden benches while Ramie, improvising, hangs back with Daria to flirt with Norm. She means well, but dear lord, is she on drugs or something? I can't be left alone with Tommy Knutson in this state. Operation Swoon is in shambles. We need an exit strategy!

Tommy sits next to me. "You're sure you're okay?" he says.

I shake some snow from my totally ruined hair and try to repeat my mantra about being a busy girl with a rich, full life, etc., but I can't focus with Tommy so close to me. "Yes," I say. "I think I'm . . . Yes. I'm . . . Yes."

Tommy nods and waits for a more content-rich response.

I try to think of something that's both witty and aloof, but all I come up with is "I hate skiing."

Tommy's face darkens.

"I mean . . . ," I say. "I mean, I don't really—"

Tommy laughs. "Don't worry," he says. "You're not the J-bar's first victim."

I giggle stupidly, then clear my throat, straighten my posture and turn away to look at the popcorn machine in the corner.

"But you are its most theatrical," he says.

Turning slowly back to him, I realize I have inadvertently launched the alluring over-the-shoulder glance. Ramie flashes me the thumbs-up sign, so I decide to go for it. Inclining my head downward, I gaze upward just past Tommy at Ramie and Daria. Ramie makes the okay sign, to which Daria nods in agreement.

Tommy follows my gaze to Ramie and Daria, who quickly return to flirting with an unimpressed Norm.

"Did you hurt your neck?" Tommy says.

I freeze for a second, then slowly, casually abort the move and return my gaze to the popcorn machine. "No," I say. "It's fine. Do you know what time it is?"

Out of the corner of my eye, I see Tommy point to a clock directly above the popcorn machine.

I laugh awkwardly and say, "Of course." Then I meet his gaze for a nanosecond, glance away and say, "I have to go now. Thanks for your help." I stand up, look at Ramie, point to my wrist and, with a head bob, indicate that it's time to go. I'm seconds from a clean getaway when I feel Tommy's warm fingers around my wrist. "Hey, Jill," he says.

For a moment, I dare to hope that the hunter has at last awoken.

He stands up and pulls me toward the smelly popcorn machine. "Can I ask you a question?"

"Um," I say. "Sure."

He releases my wrist, glances sneakily over my shoulder at Ramie and says, "What's her deal?"

"Huh?" I clear my throat. "What do you mean?"

"Your friend Ramie," he says. "She's been asking people all kinds of questions about me, like am I gay and have I ever been in jail."

"What?" I say. "I can't believe she'd—"

"Yeah," he says. "Some kids in my art class told me." He taps his knuckles idly on the splintery cocoa shack wall. "They thought she was doing it on your behalf." He smiles with only half his mouth.

I stare dumbly at Ramie, who furrows her brow at me in utter confusion. Daria keeps tapping her on the arm and mouthing, "What? What's happening?"

When I flick my eyes back to Tommy, he's smiling this

enormous Cheshire cat smile at me. After holding my gaze for an excrutiating three Mississippis, he narrows his eyes, smirks and says, "Hey, by the way, if you hate skiing, what were you doing on the J-bar?"

Gulp.

I glance at Ramie and Daria, wondering how to blink the Morse code for SOS. All they do is stare back, confused. I'm on my own here. Operation Swoon is in tatters. No abort protocol, no exit strategy, and my mission partners may as well not exist. Shuddering with another shift of wet snow down my back, I take a deep breath and improvise a response.

"Gee, Tommy," I say. "I'm not sure what you're suggesting, but it sure sounds like you have a rich fantasy life."

He absorbs my frigid stare for a moment, then looks down and laughs shyly. What an amateur.

"Anyway," I say. "Thanks for your help. See you in H Block." With as much grace as it's possible to muster in ski boots, I clomp my way toward the cocoa shack door.

"No, you won't," he says.

I stop and face him. "Pardon?"

"You won't see me in H Block," he says, "because you never look at me anymore." He walks toward me. "I'm flunking that stupid class. You were the only thing I liked about it. Now you give me the cold shoulder. What's that all about?"

"You're flunking?" I say.

He nods. "Tell you what. I'll teach you how to ski if you help me pass calculus. I mean, you were here to learn how to ski, right?"

The Cheshire cat smile again. He's toying with me!

But, on the other hand, I think he's just made a semi-romantic overture. This is good news. I should accept his offer. This is mission accomplished, right? Mouth opened, I stare at Tommy, but I can't figure out how to say yes. My hair's a wreck and I'm still stinging from my public humiliation on the J-bar.

"I don't know," I find myself saying. "I'm a very . . . I'm a busy girl." I turn away and clomp right out the cocoa shack door. I do not wait for Tommy's response. I do not wait for Ramie and Daria. I do not even retrieve my shoes from under the bench where I've left them. I crunch my heavy ski boots through the gravel parking lot and grab the driver's-side door of my Nissan. It's locked.

"Damn it," I mutter to myself. Daria has the keys.

A painful ten seconds later, Daria and Ramie burst through the door and walk briskly toward me.

"Keys, Daria," I say.

I hold up my hand and she digs them out of her jeans pocket and throws them to me. I catch them, open the door, get in and start the engine. Ramie slides into the front seat and Daria gets into the back.

"Oh my God," Daria says. "You left your shoes inside." She puts her hand on the door handle.

"Forget it," I say.

I throw the car in reverse and back out. In the rearview mirror, I spot Tommy Knutson standing in the cocoa shack doorway. Our eyes meet for a terrifying half a Mississippi, then I gun it and leave the Bump and its infernal J-bar behind me.

April 9

●

Jack

Do J-bar Jillie and Ski-dude get together? Does she help him pass calculus? Does he teach her how to ski? Are they—oh my God, I can't even say it—going to the prom?

Don't lie. Of course you want to know. You don't care about me. I'm the ugly wart on the pretty girl's cheek, remember? The Baroness of the Bump is the star of this show. Well, here's the update, ladies and gents. You know what happened after the catastrophic failure of Operation Swoon?

Nothing.

Zip, nada, zilch. Know why?

I came early. Monday morning, in fact. No time for the little princess to execute damage control. Knutsack's final image of Jill remains her frightened eyes in the rearview mirror as she fled the cocoa shack without her shoes. I wonder if he thought, *Now that's what I call a high-status woman.*

How a sensible, never-been-grounded, straight-A girl like Jill managed to acquire the requisite dumbness to get herself strung up by the J-bar is one of those perplexing mysteries.

But you know what? Entertaining as it has been to recall

Jill's flamboyant undoing, I have not spent the last three days reveling in it. Oh, no. I have had other forms of entertainment superior even to that slapstick performance. Jill, bless her, delivered the goods. Well, Mom did, shockingly.

I'm talking about porn! Lots and lots of porn. Six full-color magazines crammed with it. *Playboy, Penthouse, Hustler, Juggs, Swank* and *High Society.* Let me take you on a little tour.

Crystal, a veterinary science student at USC, has pale blue eyes, pert little knockers and light blond hair that is, how shall I put this, clearly a dye job. LaTanya, from Louisville, Kentucky, enjoys dirty dancing, pancakes and attempting to lick her left nipple with an impressively agile, if not quite long enough, tongue. Betsy, twenty-four, from Cleveland, prefers to tinker with the engine of her red Mustang on laundry day, which is the only reason I can think of for why she's doing it naked.

Then there's Martha. Sweet Martha with the wild tangle of chestnut brown hair. Oh to be that horse on which Martha lay draped, naked, eyes unfocused. What are you thinking about, Martha? Are you sad? Are you bored? Are you waiting for a hot steaming hunk of man to rescue you from equine ennui? I'm right here, Martha. Dig in your spurs and ride on over: 23 Trask Road, Winterhead, MA, 01984.

Martha's my favorite.

Not that I've given the other ladies short shrift. There's plenty of Jack to go around. At one point yesterday morning, I had all six magazines opened and spread out on the bed. Half a dozen naked and semi-naked girls stared up at me like

I was their god. What a party that was. It was better than Christmas.

But this morning, something very troubling happened: I started reading the articles. On the right-hand page, there'd be a photo of a naked girl spread-eagle on the hood of a Ferrari, and I'd be reading some blather about cuff links on the left. I was choosing journalism over tits! I've never even worn cuff links. I've never even *seen* cuff links. I'm seventeen years old, for cripes' sake. I've spent my life in one room, utterly deprived of female contact. I get three days with a stack of porno mags and what happens? My most sacred base desires conk out on me like the engine of Betsy's Mustang.

Am I broken? Diseased? Do I need Viagra?

Nope. My malady is far worse than that, ladies and gentlemen. It's terminal. It's the reason I requested all this porn in the first place. You see, these beautiful girls, naked and compliant as they may be, are no more than stand-ins for the true object of my desire. Their explicit poses and ingenious sexual experiments with door handles and produce are just lurid enough to distract me from my obsession for a few days. Ultimately, obsession wins.

Good-bye, ladies. So long and farewell. My heart and my libido belong to . . .

I won't say it. If I don't say her name, she'll have no power over me. Right?

I have her photograph hidden between the mattress and box spring. Jill doesn't know about it. I mean, technically it belongs to her. She had it taken at one of those silly booths at the Liberty Bell Mall. I've spent all morning trying to banish its existence from my mind, distracting myself with horseback Martha and nipple-licking LaTanya.

But at 11:36 p.m., after a struggle that was always doomed, I succumb to the inevitable. Digging the tiny photo from between the mattress and box spring, I sit cross-legged on the floor in my underwear. My hands in prayer around the forbidden object, I hesitate to look, knowing that once I see it, the old desire will return, potent, all-encompassing and never fully slaked.

This is not my fault. I've tried. Lord knows I've tried to squash this obsession. But I'm only human.

I open my palms and there she is.

Ramie.

Her thick, full lips pucker as she plants a big friendly kiss on Jill's face. On *my* face. Yes, I remember that moment. I remember every fractional instant of that moment, because I remember everything. Every time Ramie touches Jill's hand. Every time she whispers with hot, moist breath into Jill's ear. Every secret. Every gesture. I remember it all.

Jill pays obsessive attention to all that Ramie does and says, because she worships Ramie in her silly girl-crush way. But when I wake up alone in this room, I invade Jill's memories like a Viking horde. I mine their phone conversations, their chats by the lockers, their trips to the mall, their sharing of fitting rooms.

Oh man.

The way she bites her lower lip while she's studying Italian

Vogue, her pigeon-toed stance when she thinks no one is looking, her long slim fingers twisting Jill's hair into a French braid.

Her blue lace bra!

Screw LaTanya. Screw Betsy. Screw Martha. Only one girl will do for me. All five feet ten inches of her. All one hundred and eighteen pounds of willowy lusciousness. Body, mind and soul, Ramie, I'll take it all. Your cockeyed plan to infiltrate the student government with anarchists, your half-baked scheme to plant a bag of weed in the football captain's locker, your ambition to change the face of fashion through the unconventional use of plastics. I'm listening, Ramie.

And I'm watching too.

By 2:00 a.m., I'm spent. Drained. The porno mags are stacked neatly on the dresser next to Jill's Hello Kitty makeup case. I've got the Ramie photo in my hand (my *other* hand) and I'm staring at it by the dim light from the imitation Lladró flamenco lamp on the bedside table. I can't sleep and I can't wank anymore. It's day four. I'll be gone tomorrow. I've written Jill a note to request some porn DVDs, but I know they won't help. Next cycle, I'll find myself in this same burning dilemma.

We're supposed to keep our lives separate, Jill and I. That's the deal. That way, she can be Nancy Normal and I can spend my days watching Elvis DVDs and fighting off boredom with epic bouts of masturbation. She doesn't interfere with my life, and I don't interfere with hers.

But now, my reckless brain is concocting rationalizations.

Why, it argues, should I be condemned to a life in this room while Jill roams freely? Why should Jill get Ramie all to herself?

I know the answers to these questions. I know why we live the way we live. The world couldn't handle a cycling hermaphrodite. Hiding my existence from the outside world, cruel as it seems, is an absolute necessity. Anything I do to screw up this arrangement is an incentive for Jill and Mom to try to erase me. Not to mention, I think the success of this arrangement—especially all that Plan B stuff—is what really created me in the first place. It was only after Jill's deliberate forgetting that my separate personality evolved. I should guard this arrangement with my life!

But my devious brain won't let it lie. *Jill won't remember a thing,* it tells me. *You're nothing but a blackout phase. You can do anything you want and no one will ever know.*

For three long years (that's one hundred and forty-nine days of Jacktime, to be exact), I've endured this tiny room, mining Jill's memories for a modest vicarious existence. I've been a good little prisoner. I've eaten my peanut butter sandwiches and kept my mouth shut. But now, in the twisted logic of a sleepless night, after the porn has failed to quench my devouring hunger, I'm starting to question all of it.

Why shouldn't I sneak out that window? Why shouldn't I climb that tree outside Ramie's bedroom and watch her sleep?

It's not like I haven't thought about it. I've thought about it plenty. After Mom and Dad stopped checking up on me in here, I imagined sneaking out and following Ramie, maybe introducing myself to her as a new kid in town. But I never had the stones to go through with it.

Something's different tonight. I'm not sure what.

Getting out of bed in my T-shirt and boxer briefs, I return the forbidden photo to its hiding place between the mattress and box spring, pull on my jeans and dig out the one pair of shoes I own: ancient white Converse All Stars, which are buried beneath a pile of Jill's clothes and are at least two sizes too small. I've never worn them, never had to.

Kneeling on the pink wooden chest beneath the frosted window, I stare into the darkness beyond, then flip the locks and open it. Cold hits me with a quick and unforgiving blow. A coat. People wear coats outside, don't they?

Damn, I realize. *I'm going outside.*

I grab Jill's long black wool coat, which barely reaches my wrists and squeezes my shoulders. It looks ridiculous and—

WHAT AM I, NUTS?

I can't go outside! Someone might see me.

Nevertheless, I step onto the wooden chest and slide over the windowsill backward. Frigid air burns my ankles as I dangle a good five feet from the ground. I should have worn socks. Not that I have socks. As my fingertips strain to hold my weight, I realize that after I drop, I have no way of getting back up to the window. I'll have to come in the front door. But, of course, I don't have a key on me, and despite the fact that there has never been a break-in anywhere near my house, Mom keeps this place locked up like Fort Knox.

My fingers are about to give out when I dig my feet into

the brick face and climb back up. With a giant heave, I pull my chest across the windowsill, then wriggle to the floor.

I can't go through with this. I can't go jumping through windows and roaming the streets of Winterhead to spy on a girl as she sleeps.

But I'm going to.

I just have to do a little planning first. Jill would never go off half-cocked like this. She'd have backup plans and abort protocols. She'd have spreadsheets and pie charts. There'd be Plans A through Z and Projects One through One Hundred. I have to think!

I know Jill has a key to the front door, but I don't want my return to wake up Mom, whose bedroom is dangerously close to it. So I take the sheet off the bed and tie it around the leg of Jill's pink chest. The sheet only hangs down a few feet, so I pull the fitted sheet off the bed and tie that to the end of it. This buys me another seven feet or so, enough to jump and grab when I'm on the ground. I dig through Jill's underwear drawer for some socks, but finding only bright, girlie, lacy crap with polka dots and stuff, I decide to suffer.

Before the remains of good sense can stop me, I hang out the window and drop to the soft wood chips below.

Cold air burns my throat. What a rush.

Above me is Mom's darkened window. I freeze in anticipation of her light coming on. It doesn't. At knee height is the basement window behind which Dad sleeps. It too remains dark. After another deep breath of cold air, I slip between two holly bushes and creep to the edge of the front lawn. You can't see any other houses from here. We're at the end of a winding street.

Everything seems so far away—the giant pine tree whose branches dip into Trask Road, the telephone wires snaking away. Even the sky, jet-black with wispy clouds, seems impossibly distant.

Pulling Jill's coat tight, I look at our house dwarfed by that big sky, then turn to begin my journey down Trask Road.

When I've rounded the bend that leads me toward Main Street, I realize I've seen all of this before—the Rennies' house, with five cars jammed in the driveway, the Mazzaglias' house, meticulously landscaped by old Mr. Mazzaglia with a tiny pair of scissors—but only through Jill's perception. I know every inch of this route, yet it all feels new.

The Bukers' ferocious boxer, chained to a post out front, snarls at me but doesn't bother getting up. When I get to Main Street, not a car is in sight. I skip across to the sidewalk on the other side, then head north toward the center of town. Streetlights cast blobs of light.

When I hear a car up ahead, I tuck into the mouth of the Perkins' driveway to squat behind a bittersweet bush. The car swishes by and fades around Main Street's gentle curve.

In twenty quiet minutes, with only the sound of rustling trees to keep me company, I am at the mouth of Cherry Street—Ramie's street. I head into its dark embrace. Ramie's house is only a hundred yards in, and when I get there, a rotting wooden plaque greets me with "Boulieaux" formed in seashells. Midway up her sloping front lawn, an enormous maple extends its branches from the edge of Cherry Street to the porch roof, which creates a convenient platform beneath Ramie's bedroom window.

I crunch through the frozen grass to a splintery wooden swing that dangles from the maple tree. Stepping on it, I shinny up the rope and straddle the branch that will deliver me to the porch roof. The branch sags and creaks with my weight as I scoot outward. Halfway to the porch roof, I stop and look down. Below me is the hard, frozen ground. Above, the dark shapes of naked branches rustle and play peekaboo with the half-moon.

I am outside.

I am cold and frightened, and the knobby branch digs angry knuckles into the bony sections of my ass. I have never felt any of these sensations before. At least not with my own skin. In my three years of life, I have felt nothing but soft sheets, plush carpeting and central heating. Sure, Jill's been cold and uncomfortable plenty of times, but I never bothered to dwell on those things. Now that I'm experiencing it all with my own body, I feel electric. I want to jump. I want to swim. I want to run. I want to break something. I want to fly.

I grab the rough branch in front of me and scoot outward. When I get to the tip of the branch, it sags just below the porch roof. Grabbing the edge of the roof, I pull myself and the springy branch upward, then slide belly-first onto the rough vinyl tiles. After lying still for a few seconds to ensure that the roof can hold my weight, I turn onto my back and wait for signs that someone has heard me. There is no sound except a weak wind through the bare branches of the maple tree. Slowly, quietly, I get to my feet. Just a few strides to the left, at the corner of the house, is Ramie's bedroom window.

I won't lie. The slim remains of common sense command me to run, to stop this imbecilic mission and go back to the safety of soft sheets and plush carpeting. But common sense is the ninety-eight-pound weakling in this contest.

I walk toe-heel to the edge of the roof, where Ramie's bedroom window sits shiny and black, then press my forehead against the cold surface and make a visor with my hands. As my eyes adjust, a shape emerges, vague and cubelike. It's Ramie's bed and on it is Ramie. As the darkness retrains my eyes, I make out which end is the head and which is the foot of the bed. It's a mere three feet from this window, three feet from my hands. My breath fogs the window and I wipe it clean. I make out the tangle of Ramie's dark hair emerging like a wild bush from the pale comforter. She's lying on her back with her face turned to the window. The half-moon's light catches the sharp curve of her jaw, then fades to shadow where I know her lips are. Her big eyes are closed and a stray tangle of dark hair lies across her nose.

I am seeing Ramie's face for the very first time with my own eyes.

There is movement in my nether regions.

I want to pry open her window and slither into her bed like a snake. But I'm not that far gone. Not yet. I unbutton my jeans. The cold air is a quick dampener but my desire revives quickly. I keep unbuttoning and when I reach in, something happens inside Ramie's room.

She's rolling away from me! Instinctively, my right hand emerges from my jeans and raps on the window. Ramie starts and turns back to me. I catch a brief glimpse of the shining paleness of her face and that's when it happens.

I peel myself from the window, press my back against the sliver of roof between it and the edge—and miss!

It's not a long way to the ground. But it is far enough for me to realize I am falling from Ramie's porch with my pants unbuttoned. I do manage to right myself midfall and land feetfirst, but it's hardly a gymnast's dismount. The momentum of the fall sends me over onto my left hip and shoulder. I hear Ramie's window hiss open. Scrambling to my feet, I press my body against the porch screen and button my trousers. She moves above me, but the vague creaking is indecipherable.

If I sneak to the base of the maple tree, I should be able to see her. But then she'd see me too. Do I risk it?

The creaking stops. Either she's gone back to bed or she's waiting for me to reveal myself. I have to move eventually. I can't hide under the eaves of her porch roof all night. I guess this is what backup plans and abort protocols are all about.

As I press against the porch screen, trying to make myself as flat as possible, I recall an old Kick-the-Can strategy of Jill's. I decide to adopt it. Dropping to my belly, I snake as quietly as possible from Ramie's porch right onto the lawn, shielded only by darkness. When I get to the maple tree, I slither to the far side, then slowly get to my knees and peer around the trunk.

Ramie stands at her open window, hands pressed to the sill. The wind blows her tangle of hair and she shakes it out of her eyes. The odd thing is, she's not looking down. She's looking up. I look up to see what she's looking at, but all I see are the branches of the maple tree. In another moment, she's gone.

Desperate for another look at her, I haul ass up the maple tree and straddle the branch leading to the porch roof. I'm about to start inching outward when Ramie returns to the window, wrapped in her thick white comforter. I freeze. Ramie opens her window wide, then perches on the sill with her knees tucked up against her and the comforter as shelter. Leaning her head against the window frame, she looks upward again.

Looking upward myself, I can just make out an incredible sight between two branches of the maple tree. The wispy clouds are gone, and against the ink black of the night sky are a billion pinpricks of light. Among them, in a definite band, is the arc of the Milky Way. Turning to Ramie's window, I triangulate her gaze. She's looking right at it. She's wondering what it's like out there at the edge of the galaxy, wondering if anyone's sitting there among those stars looking earthward. I know Ramie, even if it's through the veil of Jill's perception. She's thinking all of these things, plus some things I couldn't imagine. She'll sit there until the night air seeps in through that comforter, thinking beautiful Ramie thoughts until it's too cold to bear. And I'll remain here straddling this branch with a bruised hip, frozen ankles and a persistent hard-on. I'll sit here and stare at Ramie Boulieaux until she returns to bed.

And that is exactly what we do.

April 13

Jill

When I wake up, my whole body aches. I sit up, look at my all-girl face in the mirror, then do my Plan B rituals. After that, I check the date on my clock. Friday, April 6. Seventy-eight days until prom night. Apple green marker in hand, I cross off the four previous days. Jack came early this cycle, so I have to rework my prom projections. Flipping through the months, I realize that my previously reliable 28.76-day cycle has drifted into a disconcerting irregularity. I do a quick calculation. The new average cycle length, based on the last six months, clocks in at 27.67 days. That whittles the window between prom night and Jack's expected arrival from five days to a hair-raising two! A further increase in cycle irregularity, and I could miss the prom altogether!

Prom.

Tommy.

The Bump.

The J-bar!

My life is a disaster on so many levels, I can hardly keep track of it all.

Dragging myself to the dresser, I peel off Jack's stinky white T-shirt and notice a hideous bruise on my left shoulder. Pulling his boxer briefs down, I spot its bluish green twin on my left hip. I take down the note taped to the corner of the mirror. "Hey, Jill. Sorry things didn't work out for you at the Bump. Maybe you should try something truly radical, like being yourself. Just a thought. Anyway, I do appreciate the porn. How about some DVDs next time? I like brunettes. Oh, and sorry about the bruises. I was doing yoga. Got carried away. Love, Jack."

Love, Jack? What a suck-up. And how gross is it that he knows about the Bump, that he knows about my life at all? Plus what's with showing up early? I turn the note over and write "Stop invading my phase! I'm on a tight schedule here!"

Then I realize how stupid that is. It's not as if he controls these things. I grab some paper from my desk and write, "Sure. No problem. I'll ask Mom for more naked brunettes. Hey, while you're exercising, how about trying to do something about this arm flab?"

I almost write "Love, Jill," but it feels smarmy, so I just write "Jill."

Over French toast, I ask Mom for the porn DVDs, which she agrees to after casting a cold but ambiguous glance at Dad. I have not been entirely successful in my avoidance of Baron von

Box-of-Porn, as he tends to be underfoot now and then. I suppose I shouldn't blame him for hoarding it, though. I'm sure he gets nothing from Mom. I deeply hate having psychologically complex parents. Have I told you that?

The French toast is yummy as always, but I do not linger over breakfast. I drive to school early and hide out in homeroom to avoid running into Tommy Knutson before Ramie and I can strategize damage control. It's Friday, so I just have to get through one day before a weekend-long brainstorming session can commence.

As Mrs. Schepisi and the other students filter in, I get nervous that Ramie's ditching school. But just as the late bell rings, she rushes in. Let me paint a picture for you: vintage sailor's cap, super-skinny white jeans (it's early April, for crying out loud), her dad's blue button-down shirt and a long ribbon of black grosgrain wound around her torso and thighs like she's in an S and M movie.

Eliciting the usual snide comments and chuckles from our homeroom crowd, which she ignores, Ramie slides into the seat next to me just as Mrs. Schepisi closes the homeroom door.

"Nice look," I tell her.

She pulls back and gives me the up and down. "Blue cashmere sweater set again?" she says. "Nice jeans, though. Hem them shorter. Ankle length. It's the new black."

"Along with Chubby Chic?" I say. "Anyway, what's the word on the street?"

She scoots her metal desk closer, leans over and lowers her voice. "On Tuesday he asked me where you were."

My stomach flips over.

"I told him you were out sick. I didn't want to get into the whole blood transfusion thing, but he did ask why you miss so much school."

"What did you say?"

The principal's voice crackles over the ancient PA system with pointless announcements about yearbook meetings and an upcoming pep rally for the baseball team. Like anyone cares.

"I told him you were a woman of many mysteries," Ramie says.

"Good improv."

"He did mention calculus," she says. "Are you tutoring him?"

I take a few deep breaths and release the tension from my body. It looks like, fingers crossed, I have survived the J-bar incident with at least enough dignity for Tommy Knutson to risk being seen with me for tutoring.

"You should meet him today," Ramie says. "At lunch. I'll make myself scarce so you can do sticky eyes over sines and cosines. Mmmm . . . sexy."

"That's trig, not calculus, you math dunce," I say. "How's my hair?" I turn to the side so she can see.

"Looks like it always looks."

"New conditioner," I tell her. "Hey, we're abandoning the Lexie Oswell routine, okay?"

"About time," Ramie says. "It's so not you."

"Yeah, being an uptight snob is harder than it looks. Good for your posture, though."

The bell rings and we gather our bags. As we head to the door, Ramie reaches around me from behind and tries to tie my cashmere sweater at the waist.

I push her hand away. "Stop it."

She holds tight and shuffles me out the door. In the hallway, I dig my thumbnail into her wrist.

She rips her hand away. "Ow," she says. "I'm just trying to help."

I make a quick scan of the hallway to make sure Tommy's nowhere in sight. "Shut up," I say through clenched teeth. "You've wrinkled it."

"Good. You're too perfect."

We head toward the North Wing together.

"I may be too perfect," I say, "but at least I don't look like Houdini. Are you planning a daring escape from that outfit?"

She throws her head back and rolls her eyes dramatically. "You are deeply boring."

"And *you* have a ribbon up your bum."

"Ooh, good one."

Lunch.

The cafeteria smells of spaghetti Bolognese, which is to say it smells of puke and Parmesan. I arrive early, and rather than sitting at my usual table with Ramie and Daria, I snag the table farthest from the kitchen near the big window overlooking the courtyard, with its muddy lawn and spindly cherry trees debuting the barest hint of pink bud. I take out my cheese sandwich and bottled water, then press my paper bag into a neat little mat and lay the sandwich on top of it. I want my lunch to look small and orderly. I do not want Tommy Knutson to think I am expecting him, so I resist glancing around the cafeteria. Instead, I busy myself with my sandwich and water bottle until he decides to show up. *If* he decides to show up, that is. I'm not overly concerned. I have lots of things to think about. In fact, I have my composition book open next to me and am writing very interesting things in it. Things like all the days of the week and possible names for the fashion zine Ramie and I will never start up, such as Styleslut, FashionX and Anti-Glam.

"Hey."

I look up from my notebook, and there he is. Threadbare navy blue sweater, faded baggy jeans. He's smiling at me and I notice for the first time a slight gap between his two front teeth. "Recovered?" he says.

I close my notebook. "From what?"

He slides onto the bench across from me and places his green spiral notebook and calculus text on the table next to his lunch bag. "From the J-bar," he says.

I toss out a lighthearted chuckle, which I practiced in the car on my way to school. "Oh, that. Pretty funny, huh? You should see me on water skis."

He raises his eyebrows suggestively. "I'd love to."

An outright flirtation? Whoa. Not prepared. Line!

I put my hand on his calculus book to steady myself, and change the subject. "So," I say.

He cringes. "Yeah. I thought I was smart enough for honors calculus, but my last school kind of blew. It's too late to drop down a level and I really don't want an F on my record. A D, I can live with. I figure it'll make me interesting."

I take a very small sip of my water. "I'm not sure college admission officers will see it that way."

He shrugs and pulls a foil-wrapped sandwich from his brown bag. "Not my concern." He peels back the foil, revealing what looks like wallpaper paste and spinach on multigrain bread.

"You're not going to college?" I say.

He takes a bite and shrugs. "Maybe. I'm gonna spend a year driving cross-country first." He eyeballs my sandwich. "Aren't you eating?"

Truthfully, I'm terrified of eating in front of him lest I accidentally dribble or burp. "Yeah," I say. I take a minuscule bite of my sandwich and chew as daintily as possible.

With his eyes penetrating mine like lasers, Tommy opens his mouth wide and takes a huge bite of his sandwich.

"What is that?" I say.

"Baba ghanoush," he mumbles. He holds the sandwich out to me. "Want a bite?"

His teeth have left forensically perfect marks in the bread.

"Try it," he says. "I made it myself."

Not wanting to appear rude, I put my hand over his and

guide the mushy tooth-marked thing toward my mouth. I take a very small bite.

"Don't worry," he says. "I'm not infectious or anything."

I chew and swallow, then wave his hand away. "It's great. I've never had baba ghanoush."

He reaches into his bag for a small plastic bottle of something green, then takes a swig. "So." He opens his calculus book. "Talk to me about absolute convergence."

"Okay."

Our heads come together over the calculus book as I guide him through some examples. As expected, he smells heavenly, kind of musky, like pumpkins and black licorice.

"Show me," he says.

In his notebook, I write out some equations and talk him through each step. Mostly, I keep my eyes on the notebook, but every once in a while I look up to see if he's following. His eyes lock on to mine, serious and without a trace of embarrassment.

"Nope," he says. "Still not getting it."

"Watch," I tell him. Then I take him through the steps again. When I'm too chicken to look into his eyes, I sneak glances at his chest as it rises and falls beneath the blue sweater. He's skinny, his shoulder bones boxy beneath the baggy sweater. I never realized I liked skinny guys.

"What are you doing after school?" he says.

I take in a sharp breath and open my mouth to answer when the bell slices into the cafeteria din.

"Today?" I say. I stuff my uneaten sandwich in the brown bag and put the cap on my water bottle.

Tommy puts his notebook and calculus text into his beat-up blue backpack. "There's still some snow at the Bump," he says. "Want a lesson? It'll be too late, soon."

I slide out of the bench and shoulder my bag.

"Don't worry," he says. "You don't have to use the J-bar."

I stare at the linoleum and laugh nervously. "I'm not afraid of the J-bar."

"Good," he says. "I've got to pick up some stuff for my mom right after school. Meet me at the cocoa shack at three-thirty?"

I meet his eyes for about one and a half Mississippis. "Sure," I say. "Why not?"

"Cool." He turns and walks out of the cafeteria, his blue backpack dangling from his weirdly sexy shoulder.

Four tables away, Ramie stares at me, then rushes over. "So?"

Daria catches up with us. "How'd it go?"

I want to answer their questions, but I seem to have left part of my brain in Tommy Knutson's notebook. Or it has wafted away on his pumpkiny scent. Wherever it went, it's not working for me anymore. Ramie and Daria have to physically escort me from the cafeteria to my locker so I can get my books for Spanish class.

"The Bump," is all I manage to say. "Three-thirty. Ski lesson."

Daria starts jumping up and down, and Ramie has to stifle her with a firm hand to the shoulder.

"Good work," Ramie says. "No H Block today, so the next time he sees you—"

"I'll be dangling from the J-bar?"

Ramie helps me get the Spanish books into my bag and closes the locker. "No," she says. She takes my arm and leads me down the hall toward my Spanish class. "You'll be decked out in my best ski gear and ready to face the Bump again."

Daria walks on my other side, all smiles and giggles. "He's really cute, you know. I mean, not my type at all, kind of skinny, in fact, but he's actually really cute."

I look into her deeply clueless face. "I know," I say. "Believe me, I know."

I do not wear Ramie's pale pink ski suit this time because I do not want to remind Tommy of the J-bar incident. Ramie has snuck me her mom's blue and white ski suit, which is a hair too big but looks okay after we safety pin it in a few key places. With the big orange visor, I look like an insect, but a stylish one.

Fully decked out, I sit on the bench outside the cocoa shack with a pair of rented skis and a heart that is beating so hard I fear starting an avalanche. It's three-forty-five and Tommy has not arrived. I hate for him to see me waiting around, so I clip into my skis and shuffle very slowly back and forth in front of the cocoa shack. Norm watches me from his ski rental hole and gives me a sarcastic thumbs-up.

At the foot of the hill, the J-bar taunts me.

The cocoa shack door squeaks open and Tommy emerges in his school clothes plus ski boots. He drops his skis into the snow, steps into them, and grabs his poles. "Let's hit the rope tow."

I panic.

He skis over to me and gently pulls my visor off. "I don't think you'll need that." He puts it on the bench. Then he tucks both his poles under his left arm, takes my hand and pulls me toward the rope tow. "Keep your skis parallel," he says.

There is a gentle dip over which we pick up speed and I start to wobble on my skis. He puts his arm around my waist to steady me, then stops us at the approach to the rope tow.

The Bump is virtually deserted but for a group of eight-year-olds getting a lesson from a woman I think I recognize from the flower shop on Arbor Street.

"The important thing to remember," he says, "is that you can always let go of the rope. If you start to fall, your first instinct will be to cling harder. Resist that impulse."

He stands parallel to the path of the rope, lets it run over his open hands for a few seconds, then grabs it and starts moving up the hill. Only a few yards away, he starts to wobble theatrically, lets go of the rope and falls over onto his side with his skis crisscrossed.

I try to ski toward him, but I'm not sure how to get up the hill.

Pulling himself to his feet, he skis deftly back to me. "See?" he says. "If it gets rough, just let go."

I have to admit, his mastery of skiing is surprisingly sexy.

"All right," I say.

He smiles and guides me to the rope tow. "Let it run through your hands first," he says.

I make big scoops with my hands as if I were holding a large stick, and place them under the rope. The speed surprises me as it skims my gloves.

"Skis parallel," he says.

I look down and straighten them.

"Bend your knees," he says. "And don't forget. You can always let go."

I stare at the rope rushing across my palms, bend my knees, then squeeze it tight. My body jerks forward, and a terrifying second later, my skis follow.

"Bend your knees!" he says.

I bend them deeply, which can't be alluring, but I don't know which is worse—squatting over an invisible toilet or falling into the snow.

"You're doing great," he says.

Chancing a quick look over my shoulder, I see that he's behind me on the rope tow, smiling encouragingly.

"Get ready to let go," he says.

"Okay," I say. I don't even try to sound casual. I am terrified and my whole body exclaims the fact.

Within seconds I'm at the top of the hill.

"Now!" he says.

I release the rope and the skis carry me a few more feet, then stop. Before the full horror of slipping backward down the hill sets in, Tommy's at my elbow, his perfect stop sending up a low crest of snow.

"Très smooth," he says.

Eyes glued to mine, he skis around me and rotates my body until my skis are perpendicular to the slope. Then he looks away and surveys the view. It's not exactly Everest up here, but it's higher than I thought. Smoke wafts from chimneys in the little houses on Grapevine Road, and a handful of cars, filmed in salt and frost, dot the Bump parking lot.

"Pretty," I say.

He sticky-eyes me for two breathtaking Mississippis, then says, "Ready to learn from the master?"

"Sure," I say. "When does he show up?"

"Ooh," he says. "You're going to pay for that."

I have to admit it was a brilliant improv, but it does precious little to mitigate the gut-wrenching fear I have of tumbling gracelessly down the hill.

For the next half hour, Tommy teaches me how to snowplow, which means zigzagging slowly down the hill with your skis pointing inward like pigeon toes. Mercifully, the lesson proceeds without incident, and after a dozen or so journeys up and down the slope, I conquer my fear of the rope tow.

Between useful instructions like "try not to wobble" and "don't grip the poles so hard," Tommy finds opportunities to destabilize me with his laser-beam eyes. Nevertheless, I do manage to stay mostly on my feet.

The last thing he teaches me is the hockey stop.

"It's just like skating," he says.

He skis a quarter of the way up the hill, then shouts down at me, "You skate, right?"

"I used to," I shout back. "I took figure skating lessons in third grade."

"Cool."

"It ended in tears," I say. "And stitches."

He laughs. "Watch." He skis right for me, then juts his hip out to twist his skis to the side. A small flurry of snow drifts over my legs.

"Got it?"

"Um."

He takes my hand and pulls me a quarter of the way up the slope. Then he skis down and executes another perfect hockey stop. "All right," he says. "Head straight for me."

I push off with my poles and aim for him. But when I jut my hip out, nothing happens. To avoid crashing into him, I make a wide and sloppy half turn followed by a slow-motion drop into the snow.

Tommy skis over and hovers above me. "That was pathetic." For a second, I think he's going to plop down in the snow so we can make angels together. Instead, he offers his hand and pulls me roughly to my feet.

It's dusk now, the warm reds of the sky gone blue and gray. The kids are gone. The Bump is empty. Tommy clings to my gloved hand and we stare at each other for an exhilarating three Mississippis.

Then he lets go and says, "So, Jill, there's something I need to ask you."

Okay, I think. *Stay calm. You're prepared for this. Don't look expectant. And don't scowl.*

"Really?" I say.

He starts to bounce nervously against the cold. "Yeah," he says. "Um, I don't know how to exactly . . . well, I guess I should just sort of . . ." He looks at his ski boots and exhales sharply. "This is really hard," he says.

He keeps his eyes on his boots, which gives me time to prepare myself for what I think is coming. I have to remember to act surprised, as if the thought never crossed my mind. *Prom? What? Oh, is that coming up?* Like that.

Finally, after summoning some courage, Tommy looks at me and says, "The thing is . . . What I wanted to know was, um, well, what would you think if I told you I was into guys?"

Huh?

He takes both of my gloved hands and exhales a foggy breath. "I mean, I'm into girls too," he says. "I'm way into you. It's just that sometimes I like guys."

Hold on a second. Did those words come out in the wrong order?

"Jill?" he says.

Are my ears dyslexic? Did Tommy just ask me to the prom?

"Did you hear me?" he says.

Slowly, painfully, it begins to dawn on me that he did not just ask me to the prom.

"You're . . . bi?" The words squeak out of me.

He nods. "Does that bother you? Because I wanted to make sure you were okay with it before we . . ." His expression collapses. "You're not okay with it, are you?"

"You're bisexual?" I say. "You're telling me you're bisexual?"

"Yes," he says. "I'm telling you I'm bisexual." He stares at me for a second, then tilts his head back and looks away beyond the cocoa shack. When he looks at me again, his face is darkened by pain and judgment. "I'm sorry," he says. "I don't know why I thought you'd be cool with it."

My lips come together a few times, but no words come.

"Better to know now rather than later," he says. "I've learned *that* lesson." He stares at me in expectation of a response, but I am incapable of anything but silent shock.

"I guess that's your answer," he says. Turning efficiently, he skis back to the cocoa shack.

When the paralysis wears off, I shuffle a few paces toward him. "Wait," I say.

But he doesn't hear me. Or he ignores me. The cocoa shack door slams against his retreating back and I don't ski after him.

The cruel blanket of the deepening cold embraces me.

Tommy Knutson is into guys. The man of my dreams, the love of my life, is not even heterosexual!

In the parking lot, beyond a low brown picket fence, Tommy rushes to his Prius with his skis balanced on his shoulder, achingly bony even beneath his winter coat. Something in me wants to rush to him. But I'd never get to him on my skis in time, and anyway, I still have no words for this turn of events.

I drive home in a daze. Numb, confused, almost totally blank. Then something deeply disturbing occurs to me. When I get home, I rush upstairs, peel off the ski suit and stand in front of the mirror in my underwear. In a panic, I whip out my cell phone.

"Ramie," I say, "do you think I'm mannish?"

"Huh?" she says.

"Masculine," I say. "You know, like unfeminine?"

"What on earth are you talking about?"

I turn to the side and examine my torso. "My waist," I say. "It's not *super* thin. Plus, I'm barely a B-cup. And my hips, they're kind of—"

"Jill, what brought this on? Have you been trying on clothes without me? How was your ski lesson?"

I face front and try to envision an hourglass superimposed on my form. "He's into *guys*, Ramie."

"Who?" she says.

"Tommy!" I say. "He's bi."

There is a deathly pause, during which I turn around and stare at the reflection of my ass. I always thought it was round and female. Maybe I was wrong. Maybe I was dead wrong.

"Cool," Ramie says.

"Cool?" I say. "Did you hear me? I said he was bi."

"Yes, I heard you," she says. "Bi means he's into guys *and* girls, you nitwit. You *are* a girl, right?"

I cup my left breast gently. It's barely a handful. And I have small hands!

"How much is a boob job?" I ask.

I hear a clatter as Ramie drops the phone. Then she picks it up and yells, "You are deeply not getting a boob job!"

We probably couldn't afford one anyway, but I'm not ruling it out. A C-cup. High and assertive. Jack will freak, but desperate times, desperate measures and all. Wait a minute.

Jack.

Maybe Tommy senses Jack's presence. Maybe Jack's masculine traits are leaking into my phase!

"Ramie," I say. "Please, I'm begging you. Be honest. Am. I. Mannish?"

"No. You're. Not!" she says. "You're actually annoyingly feminine, in a boring unreconstructed sort of way."

"I don't even know what that means."

"You wouldn't."

I turn and stare at my ass again. Is it the ass of a woman?

may 3

Jack

So Mr. Dreamboat's a bum bandit. Paint me shocked. I didn't see that one coming. Poor Jill. All that research and brainstorming. All that spying and plotting and scheming. What does she get for her troubles? A bad case of low self-esteem. I feel for Jill. I really do.

After his heartrending twilight confession at the Bump, the fledgling romance between them collapsed. No more Mississippi sticky eyes, no more lunchtime calculus sessions, no more ski lessons.

I've mined every waking moment of Jill's life (and quite a few sleeping moments too) and never have I seen her so low. She spent most of the first week after what can only be described as the Second Bump Tragedy doing makeovers and stuffing her bra until Ramie extra-super-double reassured her that she was not mannish.

After achieving that, Ramie tried to persuade Jill that Tommy's bisexuality should not disqualify him from prom contention. She thought Jill should apologize for making him feel mal about his sexual orientation, which, after all, is a beautiful and natural thing. That's Ramie for you. Nothing is too weird for her. Nothing is weird enough. But in the end, Jill listened to Mom, who told her over bonding cocoa one afternoon, "You know what they say, sweetheart. A bisexual man is a gay man in training."

I hate to agree with the evil Snow Queen of Winterhead, but she's probably right. I always thought there was something hinky about the guy. To be fair, I thought he was a player. I figured he'd lead Jill on, maybe convince her to help him cheat on his calculus final, then dump her right before the prom. Actually, I was rooting for that scenario. I'm not above pettiness. But seeing her all teary-eyed like that, I don't know, it does something to me. Like *that's* fair. My tears mean nothing to her. She doesn't even know about them.

I wonder what it's like to be into guys *and* girls. The thought of another dude touching my dirty bits makes me want to puke. Not that there's anything wrong with being an ass bandit, mind you. We're all very open-minded here in Winterhead, Massachusetts, the liberal bastion of the Northeast. Heck, we're the state that first legalized gay marriage. Gays are swell. Bring 'em on. If I had a life outside of this room, I'm sure some of my best friends would be homos. If there are any homos in Winterhead.

Knutsack should have just lied. It's not as if Jill had any suspicion that he occasionally dabbled in cock. Why choose full disclosure?

But enough about Jill and her self-created sob stories. I have stuff going on too. I have big, big plans for this phase.

I have decided to make contact.

The porn DVDs are all well and good, featuring, as they do, a splendid cast of naked brunettes. But they're just a smoke screen. Don't get me wrong; I've been watching them all day. I can recite the witty banter by heart.

But as night falls and my parents settle down in their separate beds on separate floors, I make final preparations for—are you ready?—Operation Window Invasion. Jill's not the only one capable of elaborate plans with cutesy names.

And this time, I don't dick around. First of all, I pick a better coat. Deep in the recesses of Jill's closet is one of Dad's castoff ski parkas. Second, I wear socks. All right, so they're lime green girl socks; at least my ankles won't freeze.

I tie the sheets together, anchor it to the chest, throw it out the window and shinny down. Then I do something I have never done before.

I run.

The night air is warmer than last time. The promise of spring is in the air. Taking huge gulps of the fresh, crisp air, I sprint all the way to the end of Trask Road and collapse in a crouch at the intersection with Main Street. Friggin' Jill. Other than gym class, the girl gets no exercise. She has two legs, good health, the expansive freedom of the outside world and where does she spend her time? In her room and Ramie's room. What a waste of a body.

When my head stops throbbing from exertion, I drag myself to my feet, cross silent, empty Main Street and start running again. The rush of cool night air in my face as the trees along Main Street blur by feels alien and powerful. My mouth hangs open to take in more air as my lungs expand and contract like a bellows. Before long, I can hear myself wheezing, but I don't stop. My rubber soles smacking the pavement beat a steady rhythm, which I try to synchronize with my breath.

Looking down, I notice something disconcerting about the way my hands pump back and forth with my stride. My wrists are bent and my hands splay outward.

Holy crap, I run like a girl!

Lurching to a stop, I grab my knees and dry heave until my breathing returns to a normal, non-life-threatening rate. It's bad enough having to share my body with a girl. Does she have to be such a wussy girl? Straightening up, I bounce around a few times like a boxer, squeeze my hands into tight fists and try to butch it up a bit. This body is mine tonight. I must evict all of Jill's lame girlie habits.

Pounding the sidewalk like a he-man now, I cross Main Street, sprint all the way to Ramie's driveway, and keel over onto my knees. Flipping onto my back, I glance up at the seashell "Boulieaux" sign. My head pounds. My chest heaves. Tiny fists punch me from the inside. How could Jill let herself get so out of shape? She used to play sports. Softball, swimming, hoops. As soon as the change happened, she turned into a daisy. Maybe the split caused it. Maybe when I woke up, she slotted all of her masculine traits into my week. How "deeply" unenlightened of her.

In the distance, a dog howls high and long. For a second,

I'm tempted, out of a vague sense of camaraderie, to let out a big wolfen howl, but I don't have the breath to summon one. As the air chills the sweat all over me, I pull myself up from the cold ground and drag my spaghetti legs to the maple tree and up the swing.

From my vantage point on the porch roof outside Ramie's window, the world is a still and inviting place. Ramie sleeps soundly, face to the window, wild tangle of dark hair obscuring her eyes. I'm tempted to rap on her window, but tonight, patience is called for.

I pull a note and some tape from my pocket, stick it to her window and shinny back down the maple tree.

On Night Two, I return to Ramie's house, hide out in the bushes at the foot of the driveway and spy. I can see that she's removed the note, and believe me, I want to shinny up that maple tree and crash through her window.

But I'm not going off half-cocked tonight. Operation Window Invasion is a multistep process.

I get as comfortable as possible in those bushes and wait to see if any cops come out to investigate. I'm no dummy. I know they're not going to park a big black and white cruiser in her driveway. I am way ahead of the curve.

You see, the note I left her last night read "Hi Ramie. Don't be scared. I'll be back at midnight tomorrow."

Now, I know Ramie. Odds are she has not called the cops. Odds are she read the note, opened the window, maybe even went out on her own to investigate, then thought about calling the cops and decided against it. Why? Ramie, "worshipper of chaos" that she is, can usually be relied on to choose the more reckless of any two options. But if she did call the cops, they're probably sitting in her living room waiting for midnight to roll around. When it does, which is, oh, right about now, surely one of them will come out to investigate.

No one does. I hunker down in those bushes for what feels like hours, waiting for evidence of law enforcement. Then, when I've had enough and can no longer resist the temptation to climb the tree and invade that window, I pull myself out of the bushes and run home.

Patience, people. The good part is coming.

On Night Three, I assume the bush position to scan for the increasingly unlikely evidence of law enforcement when, lo and behold, I see something taped to the outside of Ramie's window. Now, I'm not stupid. This could be a trap. But it could also be a reply from Ramie. With maximum stealth, I do the Kick-the-Can lawn crawl from the bushes to the maple tree and start climbing. I shinny to the edge of the branch, then stop and listen. Nothing. Absolute silence. I climb onto the porch roof, then tiptoe to Ramie's window and take down the piece of paper.

It's blank.

I brace for catastrophe. A cop is going to rappel from a black helicopter, aiming his rifle at me, at which point I will leap from the porch, twist my ankle, and limp into the arms of a SWAT team, who, after stuffing me into an unmarked van, will deliver me to a top-secret research facility for invasive and humiliating experiments, resulting in the full exposure of my darkest secrets in the pages of the *Boston Globe* under the headline "Cycling Hermaphrodite Stalker Foiled by Curiosity, Bad Planning."

Thankfully, none of that happens.

Instead, a light comes on behind me. Turning around, blank paper in hand, I spot someone standing by the maple tree pointing a flashlight up at me.

"Climb down," she says. "And don't make any sudden moves or . . . anything."

"Ramie?" I say.

"Shut up," she says. "Climb down. And don't try anything. I'm armed."

The blinding light casts her in silhouette, but I can just make out an arm held out to the side.

"Mace," she says. "And I'm not afraid to use it."

"It's okay," I tell her. "I'm not here to hurt you. I just—"

"Shhh," she says.

I grab the branch and shinny back to the trunk, spotlit the whole way. When I get to the lowest branch, I hang for a few seconds, swinging back and forth.

She shines the light right in my face.

I squeeze my eyes closed and jump to the ground. The impact sends a jolt through my spine, but I stuff the reaction so she can see how tough I am. Then, recalling that, at this point, she doesn't know my intentions, I hold my hands out, palms front.

"I'm unarmed," I say. "I'm totally harmless."

"Who are you?" she says.

"Can you, maybe, turn that thing off?" I say. "It's kind of blinding me."

"No," she says. "Who are you?"

At that point, I realize I have planned for the invasion but not for actual contact. Shielding my eyes from the flashlight's glare, I decide to dodge the question. "You didn't call the cops," I say. "Thanks."

"I can take care of myself," she says. "What do you want?"

All I want is to see her face, but the light is too bright and shining in the wrong direction. Looking at the ground, I can almost make out her feet. She's wearing black boots and dark pants. When my eyes stop stinging from the light, I realize she's moving the beam down my body. She's checking me out. Cool.

"Why do you keep coming to my window?" she says. "Why don't you just call me like a normal person?"

"I'm not a normal person, Ramie."

"Deeply," she says. "And how do you know my name?"

"Is it supposed to be a secret?" I take a tiny step toward her, shielding my face from the light with my hand.

"Stop," she says.

I take another small step. "I'm not here to hurt you."

"Stop!" she says.

I obey.

Ramie lowers the flashlight a bit, but I still can't make out her face. "What do you want?" she says again.

I sigh deeply. "I want you to let me in that window."

She laughs sharply.

"It's okay," I say. "I'm pretty sure you will, eventually."

"What makes you think that?"

"Are you kidding?" I say. "A strange but weirdly familiar guy hovering outside your window? That's like Ramie porn. Stuff like this never happens in Winterhead. Not even to you."

"How do you know me?" she says. "And that is so not true. I am deeply not letting you in that window."

"We'll see." I turn and walk away. "I'll be back tomorrow."

"I can still call the cops," she says.

It's true. But if I know Ramie (and I think I do), she won't.

Night Four. Last night before Jilltime.

After jogging to Ramie's driveway, I stop and catch my breath while staring at her window, which glows a warm, inviting yellow. Then I head to the maple tree, pull myself up the swing and shinny out onto the branch.

Ramie's dark form appears at her window.

I scrabble to the porch roof, then pad over to her and kneel before her window. Her face warped in the old glass, she jerks it open just a crack.

"How do you know the cops aren't here?" she says.

I slip the fingers of my right hand through the crack into the warm air of her bedroom, and she pushes the window down.

"Ow!" I pull my hand free and examine the indentation she's made.

Ramie closes the window all the way now, but she doesn't close the curtains and she doesn't move away.

I put my hand on the window where her face appears. "Let me in," I say.

Ramie shrugs and gestures that she can't hear me.

I don't raise my voice an iota. "Ramie, you know you're going to open this window."

Ramie's luscious mouth forms the word "what?" then "I can't hear you."

I don't raise my voice. In fact, I lower it. Bringing my forehead to the cold glass, I whisper, "Ramie. Ramie."

She steps forward and turns her ear to the window.

"That's my girl," I whisper. "Now just another step."

She faces me again, her forehead crinkled sternly. I wipe the steam from the window and stare at her. Her eyes search my face, my eyes, my nose, my mouth. Then she opens the window just a crack.

I don't move. And I don't speak. Ramie sighs, then lifts the window a tiny bit higher. Our eyes lock through the warped glass as I reach both hands under the window and yank it upward. She presses her hands to the frame as if threatening to lower it. But she doesn't. I shove both hands through the crack and wait for her to crush them.

She doesn't.

Instead, she steps away from the window.

Taking that as my cue, I open the window all the way and pull my limbs into the warm yellow glow of her bedroom.

She stands only a few feet away, watching me. Not stopping me. I close the window.

"You have to be quiet," she says.

Her wild black hair is still damp from the shower and, even from a few feet away, smells of coconut shampoo.

She was expecting me.

"Hi," I say.

She holds my gaze for a second, then looks down. Behind her, the trench coats hang like a row of sentries.

"I, um, I guess you're prepared for rain," I say.

She glances over her shoulder. "Yeah," she says. "My mom used to collect them." She backs up and fingers the hem of a black coat. "She was going to toss them, but I think I can do something with them, maybe. I'm kind of into fashion."

"Cool," I say.

I take a tiny step toward her and her muscles tense. Her eyes shift to the door, which is cracked open to the dark hallway. Her parents sleep downstairs all the way on the other side of the house, but they'd hear her scream. She's planned this geography carefully.

"Ramie," I say. "I don't have a lot of time. I can't come back tomorrow."

"Why?" she says. "Where are you going?"

"Nowhere."

I take another step toward her and her body stiffens. I'm closer to her than she is to the door. But she's not running.

As she stands still with the limp trench coats behind her, I realize the next step is mine to make. All she can do, all she *will* do, is react. Scream, run, or succumb. But she won't do anything until I do something first.

I reach for her hand. She stiffens at first, then lets me interlace my fingers with hers.

"Who *are* you?" she whispers.

Dazed by the shock of actual physical contact, I stare dumbly for a second, then mutter, "Does it matter?"

She stares back, then shakes her head, releasing more of the lush coconut scent of her hair. Her dark eyes are hungry but passive until something like impatience flickers across them. *Kiss me, asshole,* she's thinking.

That's when I realize she has orchestrated everything tonight. But furtively. She knew I'd come to the window and she knew she'd let me in, but she had to make me beg first. She had to make it seem like she had no choice.

Damn it, why do I know these things? I want to lunge at her and wrap her long limbs around me. I want to thrust my tongue down her throat. But I don't move. I *can't* move. Something vague and half buried stops me.

"Are you okay?" she says.

"What?"

Her fingers slide from mine, leaving the slick chill of palm sweat. She brushes past me to the little table by the side of her bed. "Do you want to see some of my looks?"

"Your what?"

"Looks," she says. "It's what we call an outfit. In the fashion industry."

I know this, of course, but she doesn't have to know that I know it. "Sure," I say.

She picks up her laptop and sits cross-legged on the bed, leaving a vast empty space the size of Montana next to her.

Phase Two. That's what's happening here. Ramie is evolving the proceedings to the next level without ever showing her hand.

But I shouldn't know this. These are Jillthoughts. I should be diving over the brass footrail of Ramie's bed and pressing her warm body beneath me in a hurricane of wet kisses. Shouldn't I? Instead, I walk over and sit next to her, letting my legs hang chastely off the side of the bed.

Ramie scrolls through some of her "looks" while I try to replace the noise of Jill's thought process with my own.

"The photos kind of suck," she says. "And I had to use my friend Jill as a model."

"Uh-huh."

Ramie's barefoot and her jeans are cuffed, revealing smooth ankles. She shaved, which means she was definitely expecting me and is ready for action.

"Most people think fashion is this deeply vapid label-whore thing, but they're missing its true cultural significance."

"Yeah," I say.

I wonder how long it would take to get both her sweater and her jeans off.

"Because everyone wears clothes," she says. "Even people who say they hate fashion."

"I totally agree."

She looks at me. "Really?"

"I mean, yeah," I say. "Sort of. Yeah, that seems right."

"You really don't care about fashion, do you?"

I freeze. She stares at me for a few seconds, then glances up and down my body appraisingly.

"Maybe you can educate me?" I say.

She nods. "You do all right. I like your socks."

She reaches down and pulls up the hem of my jeans to get a closer look. "Bright colors are really big right now."

I realize if she pulls my jeans up any farther, she'll notice I have razor stubble. But I don't want to discourage her from touching me, so I attempt a diversion by brushing my hand down the back of her head. Tensing, she releases my jeans and looks right at me.

I stare back.

This is the moment to make my move. She's practically begging for it.

She closes the laptop very gently.

It's now or never.

She bites her lip nervously.

The air between us is so hot with expectation, I'm starting to sweat.

But I don't act.

"Are you ever going to tell me your name?" she whispers.

I nod.

"When?"

I shrug. "Ramie?"

"Yes?"

I can feel the primal forces from deep within compelling me forward, but something else paralyzes me.

"Ramie, there's something you should—"

She leans forward and kisses me.

For a second, I disappear into the lush, wet softness of her lips, until she pulls away suddenly.

"Ow!" she says.

I've bitten her lip.

"Oh God," I say. "I'm so sorry."

She laughs gently and licks her lip. "It's okay."

How could I be so clumsy?

I'm hurled back in time to the dreaded Travis Kitterling Incident. Jill made out with him behind the dugout at the baseball field and accidentally bit his lip. He called her a vampire and everyone at school teased her.

But now I have Jill *and* Travis Kitterling in my brain, when all I want is Ramie and her luscious mouth.

"Can I try that again?" I say.

"Are you going to draw blood?"

"Do you want me to?"

She stares at me, blank-faced.

"Joking?" I say.

She nods but doesn't smile. Have I blown it? Is the moment over?

She's not moving away. In fact, she's still staring right at me. Her face is impossible to read, and I have so many conflicting ideas churning away inside of me that I hardly know who I am.

The only thing I do know is that I want to be kissing Ramie.

Right now.

I decide to start small. Inching closer, I bring my lips to the soft skin in the curve where her neck meets her shoulder.

She lets me.

I work my way up to her cheek. She pulls back and looks at me. I run the back of my finger along the line from her cheekbone to her jaw. She mimics the gesture on my face with a touch that is nothing less than electric. She lingers on my chin and pushes it up slightly.

"Hmm," she says.

"What?"

"Nothing."

She pushes her fingers through the hair behind my ears. I do the same to her. Then I bring my lips very gently to hers and—without biting—let the whole world disappear into the dark magic of her mouth. Every few seconds, I feel the tender poke of her tongue. When a hot, urgent wave overcomes me, I press her torso to the bed, the soft, yielding cushion of her breasts pressing against my flat chest. Her mouth opens wider and her jaw clenches more firmly onto mine. Finally, my body takes over. I position my knee between hers and gently part her legs. The metal of our zippers taps as I take both of her hands in mine and stretch them over her head. I position our legs and torsos so that every possible inch of our bodies connects. And all the while, our mouths explore each other, lips, tongues, even teeth touching and retreating.

When the bones of our pelvises grind against each other,

Ramie's back arches. I pull my lips from hers with a painful wrench and bury my mouth into her neck. Her arms wrap around my head.

"Why do I feel like I know you?" she says.

The sound bleeds through my body like hot liquid.

"I don't know," I say.

I press my jeans into hers and she gasps.

Pulling my lips from her neck, I look into her startled face. She closes her eyes and drops her head back.

My hand finds the hem of her sweater, then rests on the soft, doughy skin of her stomach. Bringing my lips to hers, I begin to inch my hand upward until it rests on the underwire of her bra. The rough edges of lace tickle my finger, hinting at the Shangri-la of Ramie's breast. The soft, slick movements of her mouth against mine signal unambiguously that she wants me to scale this mountain. For some reason, my hand is stuck at base camp.

She pulls her lips from mine and tries to wriggle from beneath me. I don't want to let her go, so I hold tightly and pull her over on top of me. She wraps her legs around my hips and hovers a few inches from my face.

"Can I call you?" she says.

I try to kiss her, but she backs away.

I stare at her silently until I realize I'll never be able to improvise a satisfactory lie to smooth over the ugly truth of my circumstances. She's too smart.

"No," I say. I glance at the window, imagining a speedy exit, when I realize I have a boner the size of a Buick.

Ramie kisses my forehead. "Why?" she says. "I don't mean to be boring or anything. It's just . . ."

I run both hands through her hair and pull it from her face. "Ramie," I say. "Nothing about you is boring. In fact, your non-boringness knows no limits."

She crinkles up her forehead and I realize that was a very Jill thing to say.

The warm yellow light traces the breathtaking curve of her cheek and jawline, but this only feeds my hard-on. I have to get to the window now, before I am undone by the lie-exposing probe of Ramie's mind.

"I have to go," I say.

The slow rise and fall of her chest ceases.

I start to sit up and Ramie peels her long limbs off of me.

"I'm sorry," I say.

Keeping my back to her so as to hide my erection, I slide off the bed and go to the window. I yank it open and start climbing through. Halfway over the sill, I spot her sitting on the bed, unable to squelch the hurt feeling on her face.

"I'll be back," I say. "I promise."

She says nothing as she watches me escape into the cold night air.

Jill

The next time I wake up, I have a sickening feeling in my stomach, the kind I get when I know I've been having dirty dreams. There's a good chance, however, that these dirty dreams will have been Jack's, not mine. Since I deeply want to avoid allowing anything from that mal swamp of perviness from sticking to my own mind, I rush through my Plan B rituals.

When I finish, cleansed and purified of all possible Jackness, I get out of bed and check the date on the clock. But as I'm crossing off the days of deleted Jacktime on my calendar, my memories begin to trickle in.

Memories of the Bump.

Memories of Tommy's face, that fragile, hopeful face, as he told me his secret in the purple twilight. Then I remember the aftermath. His stony face studiously avoiding me in calculus. The way he sat by himself at lunch instead of coming over for a calculus lesson.

And the way I sat there and let him.

I peel off Jack's sweaty T-shirt and underwear, then drag myself to the bathroom. I start the shower and stand underneath it despite the firm conviction that nothing will wash the unrelenting gloom from my life.

Tommy Knutson is bi.

All last cycle, I grappled with this stubborn fact, but no amount of strategizing, philosophizing or denial changed it. Ramie was no help either, despite her attempts at assuring me that it doesn't matter. She even called me a homophobe! I am deeply *not* homophobic. I didn't *want* it to matter. I even tried multiple thought experiments where I imagined myself as Tommy's girlfriend while he told me about the guys he'd dated in the past. I wanted to be okay with it. I deeply did. But my stomach wouldn't let me. Maybe my stomach is a homophobe. Why is my stomach a homophobe?

Besides, what if Mom's right? What if bisexuality *is* a pit stop on the way to homosexuality? What if I became the girl who finally pushed him over the edge? I don't need that kind of baggage. I'm over the limit already, baggagewise.

I have to be strong. I have to put him behind me. I must evict him from my mind.

As a symbolic gesture of purging, I wash my hair and tell myself to knuckle down and start strategizing a backup prom plan. If I focus on the prom, maybe I won't think about Tommy Knutson so much.

When I dry off and check the mirror for a note from Jack,

here's what I find: "Hey, Jill. Sorry to hear about Knutsack. I guess everyone has their secrets, right? Chin up and keep the porn coming."

Is that supposed to be deep? Am I receiving pseudowisdom from Jack?

I zombie through breakfast with Peter Porn and the Mom-bot, request more pervy DVDs, then drive to school in a daze. I try to focus on the prom, but my thoughts keep wandering back to Tommy Knutson, and every time they do, my stomach flips over.

In homeroom, I sit staring at the whiteboard while Mrs. Schepisi takes attendance. Ramie, fashionably late, bursts through the door just as the bell rings for A Block. She smiles nervously at Mrs. Schepisi, who marks her present with a warning scowl. As I drag myself up from my desk to trudge into the hallway, Ramie grabs my elbow.

"Big news," she says.

"Tommy?"

Her face falls. "No. Sorry. Come to my locker after A Block?"

I nod and shuffle off to history class. This brings me to the Jed Barnsworthy cluster, where the North Wing and East Wing meet. Tommy, per usual, walks toward me on his way to Spanish class, keeping his eyes glued to the dim gray tiles. I too avert my eyes, fully planning to let him pass without a word or a glance. Then something comes over me. A moment of temporary insanity, perhaps. I speed up my pace, pass Jed and his toady boys and grab Tommy by the arm.

"Come here," I say.

He stops and stares at me as if bracing for a blow.

I pull him over to the trophy case, where cheerleaders from eons past smile giddily from black-and-white photographs. "Can we talk?" I ask him.

His face crinkles in deep suspicion.

"Come on," I say. I take his hand and lead him down the North Wing toward the exit. We follow a group of kids entering the locker rooms for gym class, then cut outside into the parking lot. By the Dumpsters, a trio of cigarette-smoking goths hug their black trench coats against the still-cool May air.

"Jill, are you kidnapping me?" he says. " 'Cause my mom's not rich."

Holding his hand firmly, I rush him through the parking lot toward the soccer field, then pull him underneath the bleachers.

He shivers, then hugs himself against the chill. "She could probably scrape together a few thousand, but—"

I put my finger to his lips.

He laughs nervously, then looks at the ground, which is littered with condom wrappers and cigarette butts.

"I'm sorry," I say. "I guess I should start with that. I acted like a jerk."

"It's okay," he says. "You're not the first girl to react that way." He flicks his eyes up to mine, then stares at the ground again. "You don't have to worry about my self-esteem or anything."

"Actually," I say, "I think I was worried about my own."

He looks up at me.

"I didn't want to be the girl who made you . . ."

He stares expectantly. "Made me what?"

"Gay?" I say.

He keeps staring for a second, then laughs coldly. "It doesn't work that way."

"Really?"

"I don't see people as male or female. I just see people."

I take a deep breath and try to understand this concept. "But—"

"But what?" he says. "Don't you think the world has expended enough energy keeping men and women separate, trying to convince us we're from Mars or Venus? For what? We're from Earth."

I stare dumbly.

"We're just people," he says. "Why does it have to matter so much?"

I have no answer, only a deep, almost physical, aversion to the idea.

"Maybe I *am* a freak," he says.

"No." I stare into his kind and beautiful eyes.

The thing is, although I find the *idea* of his being into guys stomach-churningly mal, I don't find *him* mal at all. In fact, up close and personal like this, he's just as swoonworthy as he always has been.

It's so confusing.

"You're looking at me like I'm a freak, Jill."

"Sorry." I shake my head and look at the ground. Then I take his hand and lead him out from under the bleachers. I sit down on the lowest bench and he sits next to me. But not right next to me.

"Tommy . . ." I turn to face him. "I want to understand."

"Maybe you can't."

"Try me?" I say.

He sighs. "Could you explain why you're into guys but not girls?"

I stare out at the soccer field.

"Not so easy," he says. "Is it?"

"No," I say. "I just know that boys make me feel a certain way and girls don't."

"All boys?" he says.

"Of course not. I'm straight. I'm not a slut."

He stares at me in full seriousness, but I don't count the Mississippis this time. I'm too scared.

"Tommy?"

"Yeah?"

"Tell me about one of your . . ." My voice dries up.

"One of my what?" he says.

"Tell me about your first time with a guy," I say.

"Why?"

"Because . . ."

"Because you want to know if you can handle it?"

I nod.

"All right," he says. "I'll tell you about Michael Tinsley."

"Don't leave anything out," I say. "Wait, did you say Michael *Tinsley*?"

"You know him?"

So it wasn't a rich girl's name after all. "No," I say. "Go ahead."

"You sure?"

I nod. Truthfully, I'm not sure I can handle this story. But I'll never sleep again unless I force myself to try.

"You asked for it," he says. "First of all, Michael was a bit older than me."

"How old?"

"Twenty-three," he says.

"Really?"

"Yeah, but don't worry. It wasn't a molestation thing or anything."

"How did you meet?" I say.

"We met at—please don't laugh when I tell you this."

"Okay."

"Promise?"

"I promise."

"All right," he says. "We met at the Super Weenie."

I am unable to prevent a chuckle from slipping out.

"You promised!" he says.

"I'm not laughing," I say. "What's the Super Weenie?"

"It's a hot dog stand," he says. "On Long Island. It was on the way to the beach where I worked that summer. I'd go there every night to get the California Wonder Weenie."

"Okay."

He glances up to make sure I'm not laughing. "So anyway, Michael worked there. And one night, I kind of hung around the picnic tables after finishing my—" He throws me a warning look.

"After finishing your weenie?" I say.

He looks away, then whips his face back to me.

"I am so not laughing," I tell him.

He faces the soccer field. "Why am I doing this?" he says. "I must be a masochist." He runs his fingers through his hair. "So anyway, that night, Michael came out of the little shack and we kind of hung out together at the picnic tables while the manager closed the place down."

"Uh-huh."

"We talked for a while about music and movies and stuff. Then the mosquitoes started biting, so we got into his car. The front seat, not the backseat. We talked for a little bit and then at one point, he just kind of looked at me. It was so strange. I'd never had a guy look at me like that before. I put my hand on the door handle, thinking I should run, you know? But I didn't want to. He just kept looking at me. Didn't try anything. I don't know how long we sat there staring at each other. Seemed like forever. Eventually, I opened the door and went home."

My stomach, ignorant bigot that it is, flips over. Nevertheless, I can't peel my eyes from Tommy. "What happened next?" I say.

"I came back the next night," he says. "And we did the same thing, but this time he put his hand on my leg and just kind of left it there." He glances up to check my reaction. Despite the churning storm of acid in my stomach, I show none.

"We must have sat there for half an hour," he says. "But that's all we did. So I came back the next night, and . . ." He swallows. "And that was the night he kissed me."

He looks at me full bore. I do my best to hide the chaos in my stomach. "Uh-huh," I say. "Then what?"

Seeing my discomfort, he nods knowingly, then stares out at the soccer field. "It's okay, Jill," he says. "You got further than I thought you would."

"Please." I put my hand on his arm and slide closer to him. "I want to know what happened. I really do."

"Fine," he says. But his mood has darkened. "Next night, he's not there. Night after that, same thing. I show up every day for a week, and eventually, the manager tells me he split. No forwarding address, no phone number, nothing. Didn't even pick up his last paycheck. I never heard from him again." He faces me. "Happy?"

"He never called or anything?"

"He never asked for my number."

"Wow."

Tommy stares at me as if daring me to look away.

I don't.

"Do you think you were his first too?" I say.

He nods, keeping his eyes on me.

"He shouldn't have done that," I say. "He shouldn't have just left like that."

Eyes still burning into me, he shakes his head.

"You're better off without him," I say.

He nods.

We must be well beyond seven Mississippis by now but I'm not counting.

And I'm not looking away. I have survived the story. What's more, I actually sympathize. I want to find that Michael Tinsley guy and send him a nasty e-mail.

"That was cowardly and mean of him," I say.

Tommy shrugs. "It's my own fault. I don't know how I managed to fall so hard for the guy. All we ever did was make out in the front seat of his car."

Make out in the front seat of his car. *His* car. Not *her* car. It's the pronouns that get me.

But I can do this. I am still doing sticky eyes with Tommy. I haven't looked away.

Neither has he.

"Was he the only—"

"He was the first," Tommy says. "But no, he wasn't the last. If you're keeping track, my tally so far is two guys and six girls. And yes, I'm still a gay virgin. But not a straight one. Is there anything else you want to know?"

He lasers those deep brown eyes right through me. Despite the turmoil in my stomach, I rise to the challenge.

"You think I'm a jerk, don't you?" I say.

"No," he says. "I'm just sick of having to explain myself. It would be so much easier if I were just gay. Then they'd have a box to put me in. People don't understand bi. They think I'm really gay but not brave enough to admit it, like I have sex with girls as a cover."

Which is exactly what I let my mother convince me of. It

seems absurd now. I assumed that because I didn't understand something, it had to be a lie. How could I have been so stupid?

"It's not true," he says.

"What?"

"I don't have sex with girls as a cover. I really am into them."

"All of them?" I say.

"Yeah," he says. "Every last one of them."

"Slut."

"Prude."

I whack him on the arm. He smiles. "So," he says. "How'd you do?"

"Still standing."

"You're sitting."

"Metaphor, dude."

He keeps looking at me. I think we're heading for the Guinness World Record of sticky eyes.

"Anyway," I say, "being bi is one thing, but I'm much more loath to be seen with someone who's flunking calculus."

"Loath?"

"It's a word," I say.

He laughs.

"Maybe we should sneak back inside," I say. "We could go to the library."

He kicks at a Trident gum wrapper with the toe of his dirty white sneaker. "Word got out while you were absent, you know."

"Really?"

Daria, undoubtedly. She'd never do it out of malice, but she does have a tendency toward chattiness.

"Word always gets out," he says. "Eventually."

He keeps his eyes locked on mine as the cool air makes us shudder. The combination of fear and desire washing through me is a brand-new sensation. A terrifying sensation. But I feel braver than I've ever felt. Whatever Tommy and the gay leg-touchers from his past have to throw at me, I can take it.

Half an hour later, between A Block and B Block, I race to Ramie's locker, where she's trying on a necklace from the stash she hangs on her locker door.

"We need to talk prom dresses," I tell her.

"What?" She slams her locker shut and stares at me.

Over her shoulder, I spot Daria rushing toward us. She has to pause and wait for some wrestling freshboys to get out of her way. "Hey, Jill," she says. "Did you cut A Block?"

Ramie looks at me, stunned.

"Walk and talk," I say, "or we'll be late." I rush them both toward the South Wing.

"So?" Ramie says.

"Yes," I say. "I did cut A Block in order to have a chat with Tommy Knutson at the soccer bleachers."

Ramie stops short, causing Wayne and Gloria, a.k.a. the Siamese Couple, to bump into us. "You did what?" Ramie says.

"Come on." I tug her along with me. When we get to the intersection of South Wing and East Wing, Ramie pulls me with her, even though I should be walking in the other direction.

"Talk," she says.

Daria, who should be heading to gym class, tags along.

"Call me crazy," I say, "but I don't care if Tommy's bi. He's still Tommy."

"So he's not a 'gay man in training'?" Ramie says.

I shake my head. "That is such a brain-dead philosophy."

Daria skips around Ramie and walks on my other side. "But Jill," she says. "Aren't you worried?"

"About what?"

Daria leans in close. "AIDS."

"Daria!" Ramie reaches over me to whack Daria on the shoulder. "Don't be ignorant. Hey, Jill, has he actually had sex with a guy?"

"Not that it's any of your business," I say, "but no. He's still a gay virgin." I lower my voice to a whisper. "But *not* a straight one."

"That is so gross," Daria says.

Ramie shoots her a scowl. "No it isn't. It's deeply normal." She looks at me again and there's something strange in her expression. When we get to Ramie's chemistry class, we hang back outside the door while the other students filter in.

"So," I say. "We're back to the original plan, right?"

"What plan?" Ramie says.

"Shhh!" I pull them both close. "The *prom,*" I say. "I still have to score an invite. And I need to start thinking about a dress. A *normal* dress, Ramie. Nothing bizarre."

Daria's face scrunches up so much it looks like it hurts. "You still want to go to the prom with him?"

"Of course," I say. "He's going to look so cute in a tux."

The late bell rings.

Ramie squeezes my arm. "Jill, listen—"

"Don't you dare tell me I shouldn't go with him because he's bi."

"Yeah, right, dingbat. I became a homophobe like Daria over the weekend."

"Shut up," Daria says. Then she lowers her voice. "I'm not a homophobe. My cousin Sasha is gay."

"Congratulations," Ramie says. "Anyway, Jill, listen." She grabs my head, buries her mouth in my ear and whispers, "I let a stranger into my bedroom window last night."

"You what!" I pull away from her.

She yanks my ear back to her mouth and whispers, "We made out on my bed." She pulls away and looks at me. "Deets later. Gotta run. Total support on the Tommy front. I'm proud of you." She slips into the classroom.

"What?" Daria says. "What did she say?"

Ramie smiles at me from her seat in the third row.

Daria grabs my arm.

"She's lying," I tell her. "She's trying to one-up me."

"What did she say?"

"Nothing," I tell her. I turn and run back down the East Wing to art class. "Go to class."

Daria stomps her foot, then runs off.

Love, or something like it, must be in the air. In chem lab, Steven Price giddily recounts his successful attainment of a prom date with fellow trombone player, Petra Klimova, an accomplishment that apparently eviscerates any residual mal feelings he has for me. So we're back to being buds. Then, just as the bell rings, Ramie pushes the door open, all excited to fill me in with the "deets" about her window guy.

Placing the last beaker in the drying rack, I grab my bag and head into the hallway with her.

"Did you cut class early?" I say.

Nodding, she hooks her arm through mine and rushes me down the hall.

"So," I say. "Full disclosure."

"Like I ever leave anything out," she says. "Jill, when I say he's hot, I'm talking supernova. I'm talking the big bang. I'm talking—"

"Very nice, Ramie. Who *is* he?"

She shrugs theatrically.

"What do you mean you don't know? What's his name?"

She shrugs again, then throws her arms around me and nudges her nose behind my ear. "I think I'm in love."

Behind us, a pair of freshman boys giggle; then one of them blurts out, "Kiss her."

Ramie glances over her shoulder at them, then grabs my face and plants one on my lips.

I shove her away and wipe her spit from my mouth. "Ramie! I am deeply not into that *Girls Gone Wild* crap."

The freshman boys are already cheering.

I grab Ramie's bony wrist and yank her along with me. "You're such a deviant," I say. "How did you meet this guy?"

"He just showed up at my window," she says. "But the weird thing is, Jill, I feel like I know him. Don't ask me how. It's like we have this—"

"Don't say 'connection.' "

"We do!"

"Ramie!" It's déjà vu all over again. "You mean like you had with that Lansdale kid?"

"He's not a Lansdale kid."

Lansdale is a sleepaway school for boys from broken homes. Sad cases. Every once in a while, a Winterhead girl gets mixed up with one of them and it always ends badly. Ask Ramie.

"So," I say. "What did you do with him?"

Ramie gets all swoony and says, "We mostly just did, like, tongues and stuff, but he was lying on top of me and he had his hand up my shirt."

"And you don't even know his name?"

"What's in a name?" she says.

"Right," I say. "And when are you seeing him again?"

She shrugs.

"You don't know?"

"It's not a conventional relationship, Jill. Don't be boring."

"So, it's a relationship now?" I say.

Ramie nods.

"Oh, this is promising."

"Yeah," she says. "I know."

When we get to the art room, I pull her aside. "Ramie, promise me something."

"What?"

"Promise you'll call me the next time he shows up at your window."

"Why?" she says. "You want to watch?"

I poke her bony sternum with my finger. "You are a sick and dangerous individual."

She smiles sweetly. "I know. But you're the one who's dating a bi." She winks at me, then skips down the hallway, her wild black hair flowing like a wave.

On the one hand, it's nice to see Ramie take an interest in guys again. On the other, she's reached a new depth of malness in her choice of lust objects. And this guy has some stiff competition, no pun intended. Two weeks pass, and surprise, surprise, Mr. No-name Window Stalker fails to make an appearance. Fortunately, Ramie has my deeply urgent prom situation to occasionally distract her from the never-ending play-by-play of their one night of tongue action. She's even put together a "look book" of prom dress ideas for me. Most of them are wildly unacceptable, but I appreciate the effort.

On Friday, May 18, thirty-six days until prom night, I enter the cafeteria solo and find Daria and Ramie sitting at a table by the window.

"Where's Loverboy?" Daria says. "Aren't you tutoring him today?" She makes room between herself and Melinda Peters.

I sit down and take out my peanut butter and jelly sandwich. "I think Tommy's absent. I haven't seen him all day."

Ramie reaches into her bag, then slaps a big piece of paper in front of me. "My final offer," she says.

On the left side of the page is a colored-pencil drawing of a silver, pink and black dress. On the right, she's pasted a photo of a vintage silver ball gown, a one-inch square of black tulle and a magazine cutout of a pink column dress.

"It's a cut-and-paste job," Ramie says. "The vintage number is my mom's, which I'm sure she'll donate. The black tulle I already have. And we need this pink column dress, which I'm pretty sure we can pick up at Le Château for under a hundred."

"Oh, Ramie," I say.

She rolls her eyes. "I'm sorry, Jill. I am constitutionally incapable of designing anything more conservative than that. If you don't—"

I throw my arms around her. "It's beautiful."

"Let me see." Daria grabs the paper. "Wow, Rames. That is deeply cool."

Ramie pulls away and looks at me. "Do you mean it? Do you really like it?"

"I love it," I tell her. "You're a genius. The black tulle peeking through the slit and the way it contrasts with the pale pink and silver? It's inspired. It's . . . I don't even know what to say, Rames. It's like you designed the dress of my dreams."

Ramie beams. "That's 'cause I know my girl."

I take the paper back from Daria and stare at the dress. "You must. You really must."

"Don't worry," Ramie says. "I can deeply pull it off."

"I know you can," I say. "All right. The prom dress is settled thanks to Ramie's brilliance. Now all I have to do is ramp things up with Tommy."

"Right," Daria says. "Back to Project X."

"No!" I say. I look around to make sure no one's listening. Melinda Peters is trying to look like she's not eavesdropping. I shoot her an eyeball missile and she resumes her fake conversation with Alicia Bernstein. Then I lean over the table for a bit of privacy, or what passes for it in this Orwellian environment. "Project X is eighty-sixed," I say.

"Because it's sexist," Ramie adds.

"Yes, whatever," I say. "And archaic and dishonest and just generally mal. But I still need to score a prom invite."

"Oh," Daria says. "I thought scoring a prom invite *was* Project X."

Ramie shakes her head. "Did you even *read* the mission statement? Jill, how can we work with her?"

"Testify," I say. "Anyway. Let's focus here. I think the boy needs a nudge."

"Really?" Ramie stabs at a cube of tofu with a pair of red lacquer chopsticks. "He seems fairly Jill positive to me. You're doing sticky eyes again, right?"

"Yes, but—" I face Alicia Bernstein, who is not even trying to hide the fact that she's eavesdropping. "You want me to type this up for you?" I say.

She makes an innocent face for a second, then says, "Whatever. Tommy Knutson's gay."

Ramie points a chopstick at Alicia. "Bi, dude. Google it."

Melinda Peters nods sympathetically at me. "He is really cute, though."

"Yeah," I say. "I know. Anyway." I turn my back to them and huddle with Ramie and Daria. "The thing is, I think Tommy might suspect that I'm only doing sticky eyes out of political correctness. So I was thinking that maybe we need to kiss."

Ramie raises her eyebrows.

"I think if he kissed me," I say, "he'd know that my lust for him is genuine and not political."

"I see," Ramie says. "So you vant to speak in zee language of lofffff."

"Yeah, Dracula."

"No way," Ramie says. "That was deeply French."

"Whatever," I say. "How can I get him to kiss me?"

There's a bit of silence and some chewing; then Daria unleashes the following Einsteinian proposal: "Why don't you just grab him in the hallway and kiss him?"

I just look at her.

"What?" she says.

"Yeah, Daria," I say. "Then I can rip off my shirt and shake my boobs in his face."

"That reminds me," Ramie says. She picks out a long strand of seaweed and stares at it before sliding it into her mouth.

"Ramie," I say. "Please don't tell me you ripped off your shirt and shook your boobs in someone's face."

"Yeah," Daria snorts. " 'Cause they could deeply sue you for damages."

Ramie places her chopsticks down. "Jill," she says. "Why are we friends with Daria again?"

"She has a swimming pool."

Ramie nods.

"You guys deeply suck," Daria says.

I put my arm around her and give her a peck on the cheek, which, not surprisingly, inspires an improvised round of "lezzy, lezzy, lezzy" from a tableful of sophomore a-holes.

Yes, I am the subject of homocurious speculation because of my association with Tommy "the gay" Knutson. At least five times a day, someone calls me fag-lover or lezzy, which doesn't even make sense when you think about it. But since when do cranially challenged homophobes need to make sense, right? Anyway, I will undoubtedly come out of this whole affair a more well-rounded and worldly individual.

"As I was saying," Ramie says, "Mr. No-name Window Stalker is an amazing kisser."

Oh great. Another spell of pointless blatheration about a guy who Ramie spent exactly half an hour with and who, let's face it, people, she'll never see again. But I'm a good friend, so I do not roll my eyes at this. I nod supportively and wait for the right moment to move the conversation back on track.

"Jill," Ramie says. "Don't look at me like that. He *is* a good kisser. Although he did bite my lip."

"Ouch," Daria says. "On purpose?"

"I'm not sure."

"Actually," I say, "I accidentally bit Travis Kitterling while kissing him in seventh grade. It's an easy mistake to make. It means he's new at it."

"Hey, look." With a head bob, Daria indicates Tommy, who has entered the cafeteria, looking devastating as usual in his baggy jeans, white button-down shirt and navy blue sweater.

"I guess he wasn't absent," Daria says.

"Slovenly prep," Ramie says. "He needs to evolve that look a bit. I'm getting tired of that blue sweater."

"Shut up," I say. "He's perfect. And this conversation never happened."

"Right," Ramie says. She takes her prom dress picture and puts it back in her bag.

As Tommy makes his way toward us with his blue backpack slung over his shoulder, he cuts a channel of whispers and stares through the crowded cafeteria.

"Jheesh," Ramie says. "This is the longest fifteen minutes in history. Will people ever move on?"

Tommy shows no sign of acknowledging the chatter, but as he nears our table, Jed Barnsworthy, sitting two tables over, launches a French fry that soars past Tommy's nose. Tommy stops walking, then slowly turns his face to Jed.

Jed coughs out "faggot" to thunderous cackles from his toady-boy posse. I want to kill Jed. I want to smash my peanut butter sandwich in his blotchy face. But I'm too late.

Ramie stands up and yells, "Hey, Jed, when was the last time *you* saw any action? Or have you and your buddies set up a weekly circle jerk?"

In eerie unison, the handful of tables within immediate earshot peel with laughter. Then the ripple of reportage makes its way through the cafeteria.

Jed seethes for a few seconds under the expectant glare of his posse, then says, "Just don't give us all AIDS, Knutson."

While the cafeteria settles to an expectant hush, Tommy stares blankly at Jed and his toady boys. The only motion is from students newly emerged from the clangy kitchen, with looks of silent inquiry on their faces.

Extracting my legs from the cramped table, I approach Tommy through the pregnant hush.

"Don't bother, McTeague!" Jed yells. "You're not his type."

At Jed's right, wormy Paul Markusak says, "Yeah, you have the wrong-shaped hole."

Jed cackles like a hyena.

As Tommy stares at Jed, his expression changes from blank to curious, as if he could unearth the purpose of Jed's clodlike idiocy.

I take Tommy's hand. "Hey," I say. "Where were you? I haven't seen you all day."

"Doctor's appointment," he says, still staring at Jed.

"Forget him," I say. But now I'm aware of all the eyeballs sticking to us. I've never had so many people staring at me before.

As Tommy turns the full burn of his laser-beam eyes from Jed to me, I hear the low murmur of "fag-lover" and the insipid rhythm of "lezzy, lezzy, lezzy" gently blossoming amid the cafeteria's almost surreal hush. Tommy's eyes are soft, liquid, vulnerable. Despite his outward stoicism, it's clear to me now that he has no armor. Everything they say, their gestures, their curious stares penetrate him.

I try to take his other hand, but he pulls it away.

"Don't," he says. "They'll just—"

"I don't care," I say.

And it's true. Despite the heat rising to my face from all of their sticky eyeballs, I do not care what they think. As far as I'm concerned, the entire cafeteria is filled with losers and the only person worth a dime is standing right in front of me.

"I mean it," I say. I take his hand in mine, and this time, he lets me.

"You don't have to do this," he says.

"I know." I step closer.

He flinches for a second but does not pull away. When his eyes lock on to mine in that dreamy liquid way he has, I find myself doing something I never would have thought possible. I lean forward and close my eyes.

An electrifying moment later, our lips meet.

The outside world disappears for a precious few seconds, then returns in the form of unrestrained hoots and whistles.

When I pull my lips from Tommy's, a French fry lands on my shoulder, followed by a hailstorm of napkins and straws.

The heat burning my face becomes unbearable. Everyone—and I mean *everyone*—is staring at us.

But Tommy is smiling. "You keep surprising me," he says.

I keep surprising myself, I think. But I'm too stunned to speak.

"I like that about you," he says. He takes my hand and leads me back to the table, where Daria scooches over to make room for us.

A smile just shy of manic stretches Ramie's face to its limit. "Now *that's* what I call an entrance."

I sit down and fumble for my PB and J sandwich, but I'm too nervous to eat. Tommy puts his hand on my knee. "You okay?"

I nod weakly and stare at my sandwich.

As suddenly as it all bubbled up, the noise of the cafeteria quiets down.

Tommy takes his brown lunch bag out of his backpack. "I hate to say it, Jill. But I think your reputation is pretty much destroyed now."

"Really?" I say. "I didn't think I had a reputation."

"You do now," Ramie says.

Tommy takes a giant bite of his mush sandwich. "Yup," he says. "Not only are you a fag-lover and a lezzy, lezzy, whatever that is, but you're the kind of girl who makes the first move." He shakes his head in mock admonishment. "Very scandalous. What would your mother say?"

Daria looks up, startled.

"And I thought you were such a nice girl," Tommy says.

"No way," Ramie says. "Jill's like one of those people with a secret dark side. You know, like the type that goes all nuts one day and the neighbors say, 'She was quiet, kept to herself.' "

"Exactly," Tommy says around a giant mouthful. "You'll never be homecoming queen."

"Homecoming was last October," Daria says.

"Oh," Tommy says. "Well, you'll never be prom queen, then."

A deeply mal silence descends.

Tommy stops chewing and looks at me. "What?" he says. "Please don't tell me you're running for prom queen."

"You don't run for prom queen," Daria says. "I think they just kind of vote for it. At the prom."

Tommy keeps staring at me and all I can do is shove my sandwich into my mouth.

Tommy turns to Ramie. "You're not going to the prom, are you?"

Ramie shakes her head.

He turns to Daria. Daria, genius at improv that she is, faces me with a look of panic. Tommy turns to me again.

After swallowing a sticky mouthful of sandwich, I say, "Are you going?"

"Are you kidding?" he says. "Prom is such a cliché." He resumes eating his sandwich. "Spend three hundred dollars on a skeevy tux that other people have probably puked in, then rent some tacky limo and play make-believe movie star? No thanks. It's all marketing. It's nothing but canned nostalgia."

I keep my eyes on my sandwich, but I can feel Ramie's and Daria's eyes burning into me. When I finally face Tommy, all I can muster is "Hmmm."

"And what about the kids who can't get dates?" he says. "How are they supposed to feel? Being left out of this big, important social event. It's mean. The whole thing. It's cruel." He takes another big bite of his sandwich. "I wouldn't be caught dead there," he says.

●

That afternoon, Ramie and I go straight from school to her bedroom for an emergency brainstorming session. Because she thinks better while she's styling, Ramie insists on beginning construction of my prom dress while we talk. I slide into her mother's vintage silver ball gown and Ramie cuts into it with a pair of scissors. Outside, the little green buds on the big maple tree by Ramie's window mock me with their promise of late spring and all that it entails.

"How could this happen?" I say.

Ramie finishes cutting a V shape out of the front of the dress, then looks up at me and shrugs.

"If it's not one thing, it's another," I say. "First he's bi. Now he's anti-prom. Is that a thing now? Are there hundreds of you out there? Or do I just have the unbelievably bad luck of knowing the only two anti-prommers at Winterhead High? Do you think he's right? Do you think the prom is cruel?"

Ramie stands back and looks at the giant V-shaped hole she's made. "Well, he does have a point," she says. "I mean, sure; it's all magic and disco balls for the popular kids, but what about the Tony Repettos and Marcy LaForges of the world? Turn around."

I turn my back to her and catch my profile in her dresser mirror. The silver dress is ugly, but I have faith that Ramie can transform it. Not that it matters anymore. I'm clearly not going to the prom.

"Yeah, Rames, but where do you draw the line?" I say. "Should there be no dancing because some people are in wheelchairs? Should we close down all the art museums because some people are blind?"

"Well argued." She grabs a pile of black tulle from her bed and holds it up to the dress. "You know how I feel about the prom, Jill. But I'm here to support you because I know it's important. To you."

"Jeez, Rames," I say. "Condescend much?"

"Plus, this dress is definitely going to the prom."

"Great," I say. "How?"

She unrolls the tulle on the bed and cuts off a two-foot length. "Well," she says, "I guess we have to find a way to persuade Tommy that the prom is a worthwhile social event." She tucks the tulle under the front of the dress and tries to shove it into the top of my underwear. I push her hand away.

"Jill," she says, "I have to make sure I have the right kind of tulle."

"Well, don't go sticking your hand in my underwear, you perv. I'll do it." I take the tulle from her, face the mirror and tuck it into the front of my underwear. I catch a reflection of Ramie's bedroom window and the maple tree blowing in the breeze. A strange desire to escape overcomes me, an urge to slip through that window and shimmy down her maple tree.

"Earth to Jill," Ramie says. "What are you staring at?"

"Huh?" I shake the thought away, then arrange the black tulle so that it's visible under the dress. "How's that?"

Ramie screws up her face as she stares at it. "It needs structure." She goes to her closet, pulls free an empty hanger and starts unbending it from its triangle shape.

"Don't get costumey," I say. "You told me you hate that."

"I'm glad you were paying attention." She hands me the hanger. "Unravel that for me." She returns to her closet and starts shuffling through it.

I put all my weight into unbending the wire hanger, but I can't keep my eyes off that maple tree. It calls to me. I shake my head vigorously to empty my mind. "Okay," I say. "So first we outline the pro-prom argument. Then we have to figure out how to deliver it to Tommy in a way that doesn't appear desperate or manipulative."

"Piece of cake." Ramie holds up a bright pink tutu and stares at me over the top of it.

"Don't even think about it."

"Don't worry." She throws it on the floor and walks over to me. "So, what's the pro-prom argument?" She unbuttons the back of the dress and pulls the bodice down. I'm not wearing a bra, and for some reason, I feel self-conscious about being topless in front of her.

"You okay?" she says. "You look sick."

Ramie and I undress in front of each other all the time, so I don't know why it's suddenly bothering me. "I'm fine," I say. "Just cold." I shiver slightly. "So, the pro-prom argument. Well, first of all, it's an excuse to get all dressed up and look positively gorgeous."

Using a tiny pair of scissors, Ramie starts separating the bodice of the dress from the skirt. "Yeah, Jill. The guy wears the same sweater every day. I don't think that argument's going to fly. Actually, you should step out of this." She yanks the dress down, leaving me naked but for my underwear and a length of black tulle sticking out of them like a grass skirt. Ramie pulls the hair off my neck and lifts it into a loose bun. "Hey," she says. "You have really great cheekbones. You should cut your hair. A bob, maybe." She pulls my hair down into a chignon and tries to simulate a bob. "Chin up," she says.

I lift my chin.

She squints at the mirror, then touches the bottom of my chin. "Hmm."

"What?" I push her finger away and look at the half-inch scar on the bottom of my chin. "Oh, that. Skating accident." I reach for my shirt on the dresser.

"Really?" she says.

I nod. "Thought I was Tara Lipinski. Wasn't."

"Hmm."

"What?" I slide into my shirt and start buttoning it.

"Nothing," she says. "It's just that Mr. No-name has one exactly like it. Wait, don't get dressed yet. I want to try something."

I stop buttoning my shirt and look at the scar in the mirror again. "Does he skate?"

"No idea," Ramie says. "Don't worry. You can barely see it." She hands me a faded black tank top with a frayed Pepsi logo on it. Salvation Army, no doubt.

I sniff it. "I'm *not* putting that on."

"Just try it." She attempts to unbutton my shirt and I push her hand away forcefully.

"Jeez," she says. "You're so touchy today."

I stare at my scar in the mirror. "Ramie," I say. "How *did* Mr. No-name get his scar?"

"I didn't ask." She looks at my scar. "But it was exactly like that. Same place, same shape. Everything." She starts unbuttoning my shirt again slowly, gently, as if deep in thought, the coconut smell of her shampoo evoking a strange sense of déjà vu. "Jill, why hasn't he come back?"

"Huh?" I run my finger over the scar while staring in the mirror, but my gaze keeps wandering to the maple tree. If I snuck out the window, I could walk across the porch roof and climb right down. I could make a clean escape. Why do I want to make a clean escape?

Ramie pulls my shirt open and looks right in my eyes. "Do you think it was a one-night stand?"

The smell of coconut shampoo envelops me, and the room starts spinning.

"Whoa." Ramie grabs my arms. "Jill, are you okay?"

I drop onto the bed. Ramie sits next to me, and the smell of her hair makes me sick. "Ramie," I say. "I think something's happening. I think . . ." I look into her face.

She looks scared, her big brown eyes wide open and her mouth hanging slack. "What is it?" she says. "Are you getting your period or something?"

I watch her mouth, the way it opens and closes around the words. Her lips so full and soft.

"Ramie," I say. "When was he here last?"

"Who?"

"Mr. No-name."

"Um." She looks up at the ceiling. "Two weeks ago? It was the day before you came back to school. The day before your little heart-to-heart with Tommy at the soccer field. Well, the night before."

"And you'd never seen him before that?"

"I told you. He left a note on my window before that and then the next night—"

"So three days?"

"Yeah," she says. "No, four. There was one night when—"

"Oh mal," I say. "Oh mal of all mals." I stand up.

"What?" she says. "What's wrong?"

I rip the tulle out of my underwear and shove my feet into my jeans.

"Jill?" she says. "What's going on? Should I call your mother?"

I don't even bother to button my shirt. I throw on my coat, then grab my bag and run downstairs.

Sprinting out her front door, I almost trip as I hurl myself into my car and start it up. Ramie comes running out the front door, bewildered. Behind her, the maple tree rustles softly in the wind.

Throwing the car in reverse, I bolt down her gravel driveway. When I get home, the house is silent and empty. I head up the stairs to my room. "Mom!" I shout. "Mom!"

But she's not home yet. It's only 3:40. She won't be back for another two hours. I close the bedroom door and stand in the middle of the room. Scanning slowly, I look for a clue. But I don't know what kind of clue to look for.

Dad knocks on the door. "Honey, you okay?"

"I'm fine, Dad."

He opens the door anyway and hangs in the doorway. "You sure? Did something happen at school?"

"Nope," I say.

This is definitely a Mom issue.

He hovers in the doorway as if it were a neutral zone, as if he didn't need my permission to be there.

"Dad, I'm fine."

"All right," he says. "But just shout if you need anything."

Yeah, Dad. 'Cause you're deeply helpful.

After hovering pointlessly for a few more seconds, he wanders back down to his yoga hole.

Now what? How do I figure out if Jack has been doing what I suspect he's been doing? He's not going to leave me any clues. He's not going to leave me a note about it.

That's when I realize what I have to do.

I lie down on the bed and try to meditate. When the black dot enlarges around my head, instead of projecting my own face, I try to project Jack's. But I don't even know what Jack looks like anymore. I try to remember what he looked like in the beginning, before Plan B erased my memories of him, but the image is foggy.

I try a new mantra: "I am Jack McTeague." I repeat it in time with my breathing; then I take the pieces of Ramie's story about Mr. No-name sneaking in through her window and try to project it like a movie onto the blackness. I try to picture Jack and Ramie lying on the bed kissing.

1. Yuck.

2. Imagining and remembering are not the same thing.

I dive into the engulfing blackness of the meditative state, but nothing—not a single concrete memory of Jacktime—surfaces.

I persist. Somewhere in the hidden memory stores of my own brain is the true story. Somewhere in these blind alleys, Jack lurks. Deeper and deeper I dive, but the only thing the black dot manifests is a black hole of non-data.

At some point, a knock on the door pulls me out. I sit up, squinting against the sudden explosion of light.

Mom stands in the doorway. "Dad says you wanted me," she says. "Is everything okay?"

"Huh?"

"Sweetheart?" She comes over and sits on the bed. "Have you been meditating?"

"Yeah," I say.

"Why? What's wrong?"

"Promise you won't freak out."

"Jill." She's already freaking out, Mom-style, which consists of banishing all inflection from her voice to become a machine of absolute calm.

"Okay," I say. "I'm not sure or anything, and anyway, you promised you wouldn't freak out, so—"

"Jill."

"I think Jack has been sneaking out."

Mom's nostrils flare.

"I was trying to meditate my way into Jackspace to find out for sure, but I couldn't get in. I think I've built an impenetrable wall with Plan B."

"What makes you think Jack has been sneaking out?" Monosyllabic.

"You're freaking out."

"I am not freaking out. Now, tell me why you think Jack has been sneaking out."

"Well, Ramie—"

"Ramie?"

"Mom!"

"Ramie Boulieaux?"

"Of course, Ramie Boulieaux. What other Ramie do I know? And stop freaking out."

Her head makes tiny shaking motions as she tries to calm herself. "What *about* Ramie?"

"Ramie told me that someone snuck into her window."

"He snuck into *her window*?"

Now *I'm* freaking out.

may 27

Jack

On very rare occasions, the strict border between Jack and Jill blurs. We're doing the best we can here, but we are sharing a body. And biology, being an unpredictable affair prone to bizarre mutations and creative timing and all that, occasionally forces us into creepily close proximity with each other.

Take May 27.

Middle of the night. My eyes pop open to the pitch black. The red lights on my digital clock read 3:22 a.m. I want to turn over onto my left side but I can't move because I'm trapped in Dozyland—you know, that spooky state where you think you're awake but your body hasn't gotten the memo yet? I'm stiff as a corpse, trying to will my hand over my crotch for the monthly dick check. When I finally manage to flop it into position, what do I find?

A pathetic nubbin barely an inch long!

I am trapped not only in the surreal border town between sleep and wakefulness but also in the surreal border town between Jill and Jackfulness!

Fortunately, I'm not quite conscious enough to panic. Believe me, panic is called for. The last time I woke up midtransformation, the pain almost obliterated me.

This time, however, there is no pain. This time, it's all euphoria and weightlessness. Thank goodness for small mercies. As long as the little Viking reinflates to his normal state of towering menace, I can cope.

I unclench my fist to give him some room. Then I try to relax. I don't mind Dozyville. I get to observe myself dreaming, which is kind of cool.

When I've surrendered to this state, all these split-second images of people's faces start flickering in and out of existence. Mrs. Wendt, the cafeteria monitor. Jed Barnsworthy. Tommy Knutson.

Tommy Knutson?

Crap. I'm having Jill's dream. Tommy Knutson is tongue kissing me in the high school cafeteria.

Time to wrest control of the proceedings. That's the sweet bargain of Dozyville. You can control your dreams. Well, I can. I don't know how these things work for you.

So, while Tommy Knutsack jams his tongue down my throat, I exercise my directorial prerogative to demand a rewrite.

First order? Replace the love interest. Tommy Knutson is out and Ramie Boulieaux is in. In Jill's dream, Ramie has been watching us kiss from the table where she sits next to Daria, so I instruct her to stand up, walk over and shove Tommy Knutson out of the way. Then I have her grab me by the wrist and plant one, good and hard, on my open mouth. As we grind our lips against each other, the entire student body erupts in thunderous applause. Confetti and streamers rain down while the marching band, assembled now in the courtyard, strikes up "Hunk of Burning Love."

Ramie, oblivious to all the hoopla, slides her tongue deep—*no, deeper, Rames, that's it*—into my mouth.

This is dreaming, Jack-style.

I begin to slide my hand down Ramie's back in pursuit of her profoundly sweet ass when the ground begins to tremble.

An eerie hush descends over the cafeteria. A fissure opens in the floor between Ramie and me. Spreading slowly, it forces us to separate with a wet smack. Outside, the marching band comes to a stunned halt as the plate glass windows overlooking the courtyard explode. The entire student body of Winterhead High runs screaming from the cafeteria.

(When I said I could control the action in Dozyland, I didn't mean one hundred percent. Things have a tendency to veer off track.)

Not to worry, though. I am still the director of this movie. I grab Ramie's hand and jump into the fissure.

Ah, the sweet release of weightlessness.

Ramie, wild hair flowing, falls directly on top of me. But just as our bodies meet, a dull ache blossoms deep within my abdomen.

That's not me. That's biology.

Squeezing my nanodick, I prepare for the onslaught. My pelvic muscles contract and flutter as Ramie fades to translucence and is gone.

Alone now, I fall deeper into the abyss as my body completes its painful transition from Jillness to Jackness. My leg muscles elongate. My knees pop and crackle. I can feel my mouth opening and closing, but my pained screams are silent.

I try to summon Ramie. For a second, she ghost-pops into view against the retreating light from the precipice above. Then she disappears again.

The pain deepens, sharpens.

I can neither scream nor escape. To forestall full-blown panic, I try counting my breaths, but in this hellish back alley of Dozyland, I'm not even breathing.

I don't know how long this lasts, but I do know that in the midst of it, Ramie returns, black hair afrenzy. Falling downward, she wraps her long arms around me and as our wet mouths meet, the jagged knife wound of pain melts. The clenched muscles of my pelvis release, and a liquid warmth oozes through my torso and out to my limbs.

What ecstasy!

I swear I can feel it in the tips of my hair. But it's not the deep, hungry wave I'm used to. It's hesitant, fragile, as if one wrong move, one twitch, would obliterate it.

My Jackbrain, just sensible enough to comprehend things, quickly intellectualizes the sensation. I'm not yet fully transformed. Jill's girl hormones must be having their last hurrah before melting away. No sooner do I complete this thought than the ecstasy fades, taking Ramie along with it. Wordlessly, I plead for her return, plead for Jill's hormones to ripple through me one last time. But there is only the abyss and my weightless Jackbody falling.

Defeated, I relax into the falling curtain of full sleep. The fading light from the precipice closes down and I am only a moment from unconsciousness when something happens.

A tiny ripple from my core. Then an empty pause. Finally, miraculously, a hot liquid wave of pure ecstasy builds up suddenly, growing taller and taller until I'm sure I can't take it anymore. And still it grows, towering over me until . . .

CRASH!

White void!

Mind wipe.

Stunned and spent, I stare at the red numbers on the clock as they jump from 3:37 to 3:38. When I can summon the strength to move, I reach for my cock. It's back. All six inches.

Ladies and gentlemen: I, Jack McTeague, have girlgasmed into a boy body.

"Holy crap," I hear myself say. "The lucky bitches."

As 3:38 jumps to 3:39, the curtain of sleep falls.

So that was my night. One for the record books, right? Don't celebrate, though. Here's my morning:

Reaching up out of the thick white comforter, I stretch the full length of my body while savoring the luscious memory of my dream encounter with Ramie in the warm ocean of girlsex.

As my eyes focus on the window, I notice something strange. Instead of the usual horizontal slashes of sunlight streaming through the venetian blinds, there is a grid pattern. Throwing the comforter off, I head to the window and pull the blinds open.

Bars!

I shove my fingers into the grooves at the bottom of the window frame, and try to jerk it open. It sticks. At the top of the frame, I see the reason. Locks. I pry at them, but they won't budge.

Flinging open Jill's closet, I rip my jeans from a hanger, shove my legs through them and stumble to the door.

"Hey!" I say.

I grab the doorknob and yank.

It won't budge. It won't even turn.

Not only that, it's a different doorknob. The old one was silver. This one is gold. Taking a few steps back, I realize it's a new door and frame too.

I launch into it with my fists. "What the hell is this!"

I keep banging until my fists ache. "Mom! Dad!" I stare at the door as if it could answer me, then punch it one more time. "What the hell is going on?"

I slump on the edge of my bed. A few seconds later, dull voices murmur in the hallway; then a white sheet of paper slips through the threshold and bunches up against the thick white carpet. I pounce on it.

> ***I'm sorry, Jack, but you've brought this on yourself. You'll find a minifridge in your bathroom with plenty of food for four days. If you***

need anything else, just slip a note through the door.

Love, Mom and Dad

It's printed on Mom's personal letterhead. The robot sat down at her laptop, opened her Helen McTeague letterhead and composed a memo to me.

I crumple it in my fist and throw it at the door. It connects with a pitiful slap and drifts to the floor.

How did this happen? *Why* did this happen? How did they find out about . . .

It all comes stampeding back.

The scar.

I stare at the door while the murmuring in the hallway rises, falls, then ends abruptly. One set of footsteps retreats down the hallway. I go to the window, still naked.

Outside, Mom descends the front steps. I bring the meat of my fist to the window with a dull thud. She stops, briefcase in hand, but doesn't turn around.

"Let me out!" I scream.

Straightening her shoulders, she casually resumes walking to her stupid beige Saab.

I punch the window, knuckles first, but the glass must be bulletproof. It's probably soundproof too. Not that there's anyone to hear me out here. Our house is the only one at the end of this winding road.

For a few seconds, Mom watches me from behind the wheel, then shifts to reverse and pulls out.

I run to the door and start banging. "Dad!" I scream. "Dad!"

A few seconds later, a pencil worms through the threshold. Uncrinkling Mom's note, I stab out the words "Let me out!" then slide it through. About twenty seconds later, it comes back. Underneath my writing, Dad has written,

I'm sorry, Jack. I'm really sorry.

Love, Dad

PS: Happy birthday, kiddo

I stand up and look at Jill's dork calendar. Sure enough, it's May 28, our eighteenth birthday. To celebrate the festive occasion, I scribble every obscenity I can think of on Dad's little note, but I don't send it through. What's the point? Maybe he'll slide a piece of birthday cake under the doorjamb later and I can sing "Happy Birthday," then set myself on fire. I slump to the floor and stare at Dad's handwriting.

Dad. What a joke. He's barely Dad anymore. He's barely *human* anymore. For better or worse, I can tap into all of Jill's childhood memories, so I can recall a time when Dad was actually a cool guy. Back when Jill was just a normal little girl, he'd come home from the office in his blue suit and change into sweatpants so they could shoot hoops in the driveway with her pink Barbie net. He taught her how to do a layup. He used to tell gross jokes at the dinner table and laugh with her while Mom pursed her lips in distaste.

Somewhere along the line, that guy died and Yogi Useless was born. I don't know what killed him. His job? Mom? Me?

Maybe all three. Maybe Mom and the job crippled him and I finished him off. Jill used to hear them arguing, but she was too young to know what "partnership" meant. A partner was something you had in gym class.

The thing is, if it weren't for Mom and her God-like control of everything that transpires in this fiefdom, Dad probably *would* help me.

Dad opposed Plan B in the beginning. He only went along with it because Mom insisted. It was insidiously ingenious of Mom to incorporate Dad's meditation into it. That made Plan B his baby too. What a sucker.

Slumped on the floor, holding this memo from Mom and this pathetic handwritten apology from Dad, I'm so full of self-pity I want to shoot myself. Too bad they haven't left me a gun. That would teach them. The look on Mom's face when she found my dead body. It would almost be worth it. There's Plan B for you, Helen. Hope you're happy now.

I stand up and pace in front of my bed for a while, then go to the bathroom and open the minifridge they've perched on Jill's wrought-iron chair. Let's see what culinary delights I have to look forward to. A half-gallon of organic milk, two pints of orange juice (with pulp), half a pound of roast beef, half a pound of American cheese, some yogurt, some peeled baby carrots and a tomato. On the bathroom counter next to Jill's array of a zillion useless skin-care products are a loaf of whole wheat bread, a box of Grape-Nuts, two bags of potato chips and a jar of Skippy peanut butter. Chunky! The bitch knows I like smooth.

This is what I've become to them. A shopping list.

In the cabinet under the sink, between a box of tampons and a pink plastic bucket filled with yet more pointless hygiene products, are a bowl, a dish, a glass, a fork, a knife and a spoon. Oh, and isn't this thoughtful: miniature salt and pepper shakers so that I can properly season my prison food.

I want to puke.

I want to kill somebody, then puke.

No. I want to kill somebody, puke, then die.

I slump onto the white wicker bench crammed under the towel rack and stare at the slow drip from the bathtub faucet. Every possible inch of horizontal surface is occupied by shampoo, conditioner, exfoliant, moisturizer or gel—all in different colors and smells. What a life this girl has. Every day, her biggest problem is choosing which type of fruit she wants to smell like. Why do girls want to smell like fruit, anyway? Are guys supposed to find that sexy?

What does Ramie smell like? Oh yeah, coconut. But only her hair. Her skin smells of . . . hmmm, what is it, exactly? Vanilla? No. It's something more animal, more . . .

I want to die! I can't live like this. I know I've voluntarily confined myself to this room for three years, but it's different now. I've tasted freedom. I've tasted Ramie's lips. I can't go back to the old ways, resigned to a vicarious life of obsessive recall. I need the outside air. I need Ramie's maple tree. I need Ramie!

My eyes fall on a cluster of beauty implements bunched into

a small white coffee cup on the counter. Tweezers, makeup brushes, a nail file, a tiny pair of nail scissors.

Nail scissors.

I rush to them and flick them open and shut. Staring into the mirror, I watch as my sad face comes alive with a new sense of purpose. A guy could do a lot of damage with nail scissors.

A lot of damage.

JUNE 1

Jill

"Aaaaaahhhhhhh!"

Metal on metal. The clatter and cachink of the new lock. Then the bedroom door flies open and Dad rushes in.

"Sweet Jesus," he says.

Mom rushes in still wet from the shower and wrapping a towel around herself. "What's going—" She freezes when she sees me, her hair fizzing with shampoo. "What happened to your—" She comes at me slowly, wet arms outstretched as if she were preparing to capture a dangerous moth. "Are you hurt?"

"I . . . I . . ."

I can't take my eyes off the mirror.

"Jill, honey?" she says.

"I haven't done Plan B yet, Mom. I still remember— Oh mal!"

Him! Jack. The nail scissors!

I cover my face with my hands. Peering between two fingers, I look at the mirror again. It's still there. That hideous, mal thing is staring back at me with my own eyes.

"It's okay," Mom says.

"It's not okay!" I say.

Dad chews violently on his thumbnail. "What should we do?" he says. "Helen, what do we do?"

Mom turns on him like a viper. "Shut up." Then she faces me with a forced calm. "It's okay. Let me just have a closer look." She kneels on the edge of the bed, pulling her towel up with her. She inspects my neck and arms, then pulls the covers down over my naked torso. In the doorway, Dad turns and starts pacing just outside in the hallway. Mom looks up and down my legs. "Are you hurt anywhere, sweetie?"

I shake my head. "I don't think so."

She steps off the bed, holding her towel closed, and has another look at me, trying—and totally failing—to appear unfazed. "Everything looks okay," she says.

"Everything does *not* look okay, Mom." I face the mirror again. "Look at me!"

"Shhh," she says. "Jill. Listen to me. Jill."

I pull my eyes away from the ghoulish creature staring at me in the mirror.

"Jill," she says. "I want you to do Plan B. Okay?"

"But—"

Mom puts her hands on my shoulders. "You can do it, honey. Look in the mirror."

I look in the mirror again. Staring back is indeed my face. My girl face, my girl eyes, my girl nose and mouth. But something's missing.

Most of my hair.

Cruel shingles of it poke from the right side of my head.

On the left, I am almost completely bald except for a cluster of scabby wounds where Jack cut it so close he nicked my scalp.

Panic rises like bile, but I keep staring at my reflection. I do not look at my parents in the edges of my peripheral vision. I focus on my eyes. That's what matters. Not this scabby head.

When I've taken in the image, I lie down and close my eyes.

"I am all girl," I say.

The black dot pops into view in the center of my forehead. I love that dot. Sometimes I think it's the only reliable thing in my life. I repeat the mantra as the black dot expands; then I project Jack's four days onto the blackness.

His face, his hands, the nail scissors.

"I am all girl."

The crisp image of his hair falling into the damp sink.

"I am all girl."

The beads of sweat on his determined face, the stink of his armpits as he paces the room.

"I am all girl."

His hunger, his hard-on, his longing for Ramie.

"I am all girl."

His rage, his envy, his lust.

"I am all girl."

All of it projected like a scary movie until I fade it all the way to black.

I let the blackness calm me for a moment; then I project my

own face onto it. It's frightened, butchered, but most importantly, all girl.

When I've absorbed it in all of its pure femininity, I open my eyes and stare at the ceiling. He's gone. All of him. Even his dreams.

We don't bother with French toast this morning. Instead, Mom cuts off the hair on the right side of my head to even it out. Then she digs out the Yellow Pages and flips it open to the wig page.

Meanwhile, Dad comes up from the basement holding a disgusting trucker cap that reads "#1 Dad." "I found this," he says. "Until you get the right wig."

Mom and I look at each other.

"No good?" he says.

"Richard," Mom says. "Why don't you go upstairs and grab Jill's pink hoodie sweatshirt, which is usually hanging from a hook on the inside of her closet."

"But Mom," I say. "I never wear the hood up. I'll look like a girl gangster."

"It's temporary," she says. "Richard?"

Dad faces me with that "poor little dear" look, then rushes upstairs.

Mom runs her finger down the list of wig stores, then rips the whole page out.

"Where are we going?" I say.

"Burlington," she says.

"Not the Burlington mall," I say. "We could deeply run into someone there."

"It's not at the mall," she says. "And it's Friday morning. We're not going to run into anyone."

Dad comes back and hands me my pink hoodie. The soft fuzzy underside pulls at the scabs on my head. I check out my reflection in the microwave door. "I should put on some makeup."

Mom scrutinizes me, then nods. I run upstairs, grab my makeup bag and decide to put it on in the car.

Dad doesn't come with us. I can't remember the last time he left the house. I think he's becoming agoraphobic, but now is not the time to ponder such freakitudes. Mom and I drive down Main Street in the opposite direction of the high school. Never taking her steely gaze from the road, Mom digs around in her purse for a stick of gum. She always chews gum when she's nervous.

I flip the visor down and look at my hideous head in the mirror. "I look like a mental patient," I say. "How can I face Tommy looking like this?"

Mom chomps her gum. "You're *not* going to look like this, honey. You're getting a wig, and everything will be fine."

Fine. Sure, everything will be *fine*. Everything's always *fine*. I think Mom believes that if she keeps insisting on this delusion, one day it will come true.

I am not so deluded.

I examine one of the scabs on the left side of my head.

"Mom," I say. "Do you think Jack intentionally cut into the skin, or do you think he was just trying to cut the hair too close?"

"Let's not overanalyze what Jack does," she says. "The important thing is containment."

I flip the visor back up. "Yeah, Mom, but we don't have containment. He may be locked up in my room, but what's to prevent him from doing something else? Something worse?"

Mom chomps her gum like it's the last piece on earth.

"Tranquilizers," she says.

"What?"

She narrows her eyes at the road.

"Mom, are you serious?"

Chew, chomp. Chew, chomp.

"Wouldn't that be kind of dangerous?" I say.

Mom glances at me for a second, then returns her eyes to the road. "I'll look into it, honey."

By "look into it," she means she'll test them on herself first, like she did with that estrogen stuff.

"No, Mom," I say. "No way."

Chew, chomp. Chew, chomp.

Besides—and I don't say this part out loud—something about it seems wrong. Tranquilizing Jack is tantamount to murdering him. He doesn't deserve that, does he?

Does he?

"Mom," I say. "Promise me you're not going to start experimenting with tranquilizers."

Mom puts her hand on my knee. "Don't worry, honey. I'll slip them into Dad's jasmine tea first."

"Mom!"

"I'm kidding."

Up ahead is a sign for Route 114. With maximum efficiency, she signals and merges right, her jaw making mincemeat of that poor stick of gum.

The lady in the first wig store is about one hundred years old and deeply in love with the 1950s. Almost every wig is brunette and styled in a bouffant, including the one she's wearing. Mom and I try out a couple and realize there is no way I can pull off a single one of them unless I want to look like Annette Funicello.

The next store is in a strip mall in Saugus and features mostly bright pink, blue and neon green costume wigs. At the end of one narrow aisle is a single long, straight, brown wig that looks vaguely normal. Mom tugs me toward it, then lifts it from its mannequin head and puts it on me. Hands on my shoulders, she guides me to a dirty heart-shaped mirror hanging crookedly from a metal post. I can barely get far enough away from it to see. Way-too-loud techno music blares at us.

"I think it's the wrong color," I say.

Mom exhales through her nose, then approaches the goth store clerk slumping by the cash register.

"Can that one be dyed?"

The goth clerk mouths "What?" through black lips.

Mom raises her voice and asks again.

The girl shakes her head.

I take it off and place it back on the mannequin. Crooked. On purpose. I swear the whole place smells like marijuana.

Mom waits for me by the door, holds it open, then says "thank you" to the girl in a tone that completely reverses its meaning.

In the strip mall parking lot, I sit in the passenger seat, staring at Route 1. Every car whizzing by makes me sink deeper into my hoodie. With the torn-off sheet from the Yellow Pages in her lap, Mom starts calling every wig store on the North Shore with detailed questions.

While she does this, I put my feet up on the dashboard and try to figure out what exactly Jack was hoping to accomplish with this "haircut." I mean, obviously, he was acting out because we locked him in the bedroom. But did he honestly think we'd react by setting him free? Is this some kind of deluded brinkmanship? I thought he was on board with our arrangement. He's never complained about it before. All of a sudden, he's stalking my best friend and cutting off my hair. What's that about?

Maybe I shouldn't have "deleted" him so quickly after I woke up. Maybe I should have allowed my memory to wander into Jacktime a little. Know your enemy, and all that. When did Jack become my enemy?

"Thirty-two Franklin Street?" Mom says into the phone. "Off of Boylston?" Shoving the cell phone between her ear and shoulder, she snaps her fingers and points to the glove compartment.

I dig out the atlas.

"All right," she says into the phone. "And you're sure you have a natural-looking medium-brown to auburn wig? Straight?" She nods. "Okay. I'll be there in twenty minutes." She hangs up and looks at me. "This is not going to be cheap." She folds the torn-off Yellow Pages sheet and slips it into her purse. "And we have to go to Boston." She says "Boston" the way someone else would say "hell."

"Really?" I say.

She nods, then reverses the Saab out of its spot. "Whatever it takes," she says. "We can sell it on eBay when your hair grows back."

"Uh-huh," I say.

We wait forever at the exit until there's a gap between two cars just wide enough to rocket between. I pull my pink hoodie down low, over my eyebrows, nearly over my eyes.

Technically, the strip mall we've just departed is only fifteen minutes from Theatrical Features, a.k.a. "the wig store," in Boston. But this is Boston, after all, so it takes us a full two hours to find the place. Mom hates—I mean *hates*—driving in Boston, and I don't blame her. Whoever designed these streets was clearly on crack. It's amazing that there are enough smart people here to fill up Harvard and MIT. Oh, and don't bother asking anyone for directions. Giving strangers confusing, vague or intentionally wrong directions is Boston's number one hobby. After circling Government Center four times in search of Franklin Street, Mom pulls into the nearest parking garage and we decide to walk the rest of the way.

As soon as we emerge from the cool, dark garage into the sunlit, jam-packed sidewalks of Government Center, I want to curl up and die. I know no one can tell I'm butchered and scabby under my pink hoodie, but I feel like such a dork. Mom asks a cop to direct us to Franklin Street. It's three left turns, followed by a right turn, a circle, a square and a squiggle. Eventually, we find the entrance to Theatrical Features in the side of an old brick warehouse. Mom takes my hand and we wait in the dark entrance, where shelves overflow with gloves, hats and a gazillion other accessories. Hearing the entrance bell, a thirtyish gay guy steps out from behind a counter displaying about six hundred types of black leather gloves.

"Hi," he says. "These aren't for sale or rent," he explains. "It's my personal collection."

Mom smiles her manic robot smile as if it will protect her from this guy's flamboyant homosexuality. She's not a homophobe or anything. It's just that whenever she meets anyone who is in any way outside of the norm, she makes such a huge effort of not noticing or judging that it becomes obvious that she's noticing and judging. Me, on the other hand? I'm dating a bisexual guy, so I'm not even fazed by this.

"What can I do for you?" he says.

"I called about the wigs?" Mom says. "Natural hair, medium brown to auburn?"

"Ah." He claps his hands and looks around as if in search of a nearby display of wigs. "I'm Charles, by the way."

Mom nods.

He puts his very small hand very gently on Mom's shoulder.

"Have a seat. I'll be right back." He gestures like a game show host to two ancient wingback chairs tucked under and somehow into a display of giant candy canes. Then he rushes off down a corridor jammed on either side with ball gowns, riding crops, cowboy boots, baseball hats and every type of petticoat you could ever need. If you needed that kind of thing. The whole place is one sneeze away from a costume avalanche.

Mom sighs, then sits down. "I think we'll find what we need here."

A few minutes later, Charles returns through a different corridor, his left hand draped with what looks like a wet muskrat.

"Here we go," he says. He stands in front of us and presents the thing on his fist, bangs front. "Now, you're going to be putting this on yourself, I take it?" He cocks his head and purses his lips as he looks at me. He probably thinks I'm a cancer patient. "Listen." He runs his slender fingers through the thick brown bangs. "Bangs," he says. "Bangs are essential unless you're very adept at placement." He examines my face from side to side. "You've got a cute nose, so you can wear bangs. Let's give it a try."

I pull the hoodie off my scabby head.

Trying valiantly to hide his curiosity, he removes a thin mesh skullcap from the black nylon utility belt he's put on. "Why don't you put this on first?"

I try to stretch it from front to back, but it keeps snapping back. Mom holds one end of it and we spread it out above my head.

"That's it," he says. "You need to be able to do this on your own. Now, watch the ears."

I guide it down to just above my eyebrows and pull it into place.

"Excellent." He adjusts it back a bit on my forehead, then fits the wig on top of it.

The color is pretty close to my natural color, if less mousy. It's a shortish bob with heavy bangs.

Mom has a look and nods approvingly. "Not bad," she says.

"It's not too frumpy, is it?" I say. "I don't want to look like a soccer mom."

"Soccer mom?" Charles removes a long, thin metal comb from his utility belt. "Please. Did you see *Chicago*? It's practically Velma." Very carefully, he combs out some tangles.

I look at myself in the mirror and have to admit there's a sort of vintage chic to it.

"You like it, honey?" Mom says.

There's a softness in her voice. She's relieved. We've won this round. We've beaten Jack, my brand-new enemy.

"Yeah," I say.

Then I look at Charles, who's eyeballing the wig in search of microtangles to vanquish with his surgical comb.

"Thanks," I say.

"Oh, don't be silly," he says with a wink. "Wigs are what we do."

The whole way home, I stare at myself in the mirror, pushing my seat as far back as possible to take in the full shape of my head.

"It makes me want to do jazz hands, Mom."

Mom sneaks a quick look at me, then merges onto Route 114.

"It's classic," she says. "It's a style that never goes out of style."

I turn to the side to examine my profile. "It doesn't make my nose look big, does it? You know, the bangs?"

"You don't have a big nose, sweetie. I'm a little concerned about your mouth, though."

I face the mirror full on. It's true. I have a big mouth. That's why I wear my hair layered. Thing is, I've never minded my big mouth. I think there's something kind of cool about it.

I purse my lips, then smile wide. I've never looked so not me. "I like it," I tell her.

"When we get home," Mom says, "I want to put it through some tests. Make sure it's secure."

I still can't peel my eyes from the mirror. "Does it look like real hair?"

"It *is* real hair."

"But does it *look* like real hair?"

She turns onto Trask Road and pulls over for a second. Then she faces me with a scientist's eye. "It does," she says.

We head down Trask Road toward our house and who do we spot sitting on the cement flower bed at the top of the steps, drinking something from a cruddy jam jar with Dad?

Ramie.

"Mom," I say. "Drive past. Drive past!"

"What?" she says.

But it's too late. Both Ramie and Dad have spotted us.

Mom pulls into the driveway and turns off the ignition. "It's okay," she says. "We went to the mall and had your hair colored and cut. That's why it looks different. Don't worry. We can do this."

But it's not the wig that worries me. It's Ramie.

"Honey," Mom says. "What's wrong?"

Her face morphs into slow understanding. "Oh," she says. "Do you remember? Are you remembering what they—"

"No," I say. "I don't remember. It's just . . ."

Ramie stands up with her jam jar and waves, her short flared skirt blowing all the way up to her thighs.

"I feel sick, Mom."

"It's okay," Mom says. "You go inside. You don't stop. I tell her you're not well. She goes home. End of story."

"I think I'm going to puke," I say.

"Good." Mom grabs her purse and puts her hand on the door handle. "Then you won't have to act."

Dad stands up next to Ramie with a dumb smile on his face, as if Ramie's arrival were good news. He's such an idiot sometimes.

Mom opens her door. "Not a word to her, understand? Just go inside and let me handle it."

We get out of the car and close the doors in near-perfect synch. Mom heads up the walkway in front while I try to hide behind her. Ramie twists and turns to catch a glimpse of me.

"Hey, sexy!" she yells.

My stomach flips over. Reaching back, Mom grabs my wrist

and pulls me up the stairs, keeping herself between Ramie and me.

When we get to the top of the stairs, Dad's still smiling his idiot grin. "Don't you look elegant," he says.

Mom stops, placing her body directly between Ramie and me while dragging me by the wrist toward the door. Keeping my eyes on the blue and pink flagstones at the top of the landing, all I see of Ramie is her bony ankles. I fumble with the sticking screen door and slip inside. From inside the vestibule, I hear Mom say, "Jill's not feeling well, Ramie. She needs to lie down. Richard?"

I turn to face the door and Ramie peers around my mom's formidable buffer of a body with a perplexed look on her face. The brief second our eyes meet feels like a swarm of hornets stinging me all at once. I turn and run up the stairs.

When I get to my room, I'm afraid to go to the window, because I know Ramie can see me from the front steps. So I drop to my knees, crawl to the wooden chest and peer over the windowsill between the bars. Mom ushers a chastened Dad inside while Ramie heads down the stairs. She pulls her rusty old ten-speed from the bushes where she always dumps it, stands it upright and looks up at my window. I pull back and hide. A breeze blows her hair as she stares up at me, surprised, probably, by the bars on the window. Then she turns the bike around, straddles it and rides off, her flimsy skirt fluttering up to reveal a black lace thong.

My stomach flips over again.

Having redeposited Dad into his yoga hole, Mom comes

to my room and hovers in the doorframe. "Shake your head," she says.

"What?"

She demonstrates by shaking her head side to side.

I do it.

"Feel secure?" she says.

"I guess." I tug at the ends of the bob. "I don't know if it'll survive gym class."

"I'll write you a note," she says. "You can forget about gym class for the rest of the year."

"Really?"

She nods. She hovers.

"What?" I say.

"Do I even have to say it?"

"Say what?"

She steps inside and leans against my desk, arms folded businesslike across her chest. "Look," she says. "You've always been a loyal friend, but I think it's time to reexamine your relationship with—"

"Mom." I press my fingers into my eye sockets. "Please. Let's not talk about Ramie."

Mom doesn't say anything, but she keeps staring at me like she can't wait to use this latest humiliation to banish Ramie from my life. Right now, I'm not inclined to defend Ramie, but I don't want to talk about her. Even the sound of the word "Ramie" nauseates me in a deeply unfamiliar way.

"I'm going to lie down for a while," I say. "I think I need a nap."

"Sure," she says. But she keeps hovering.

"What?"

She presses her lips into a neat little smile. "Dad's right, honey. It *is* elegant."

I glance in the mirror again. "Really?"

She nods, then leaves.

As soon as I lie down, my cell phone rings. It's Ramie. She'll keep calling until I pick up, so I shut the phone off. Then I stare at the calendar, where the word "PROM!" appears in red letters at the bottom of the month.

When I get to school on Monday, instead of going to homeroom, I hide out in a stall in the girls' room. The last thing I need on my first day back is to face Ramie and her lie-exposing mind probe. The only lie I've ever told her is the Big One about my "blood transfusions." We made a "pinkie promise" back in middle school to tell each other everything. She, of course, responded by unloading a catalog of perverted sex stuff and I told her about how I let Christopher Defoe touch my boob in sixth grade. We've been BFFs ever since. But right now, the thought of Ramie makes me feel all creepy inside, like I've done something unforgivably wrong. And though I have no direct memory of her pervy gropings with Jack, Ramie's descriptions have been gut-wrenchingly explicit. What's more, I think somehow my body remembers it, even though my brain doesn't. Does that make sense?

So anyway, I hide out in the girls' room until I hear the bell for A Block; then I pop my head into homeroom and wave at Mrs. Schepisi.

"I'm going to have to mark you late, Jill," she says.

When I've recovered from the shock of that threat, I slip back into the hallway and speed walk toward history class.

"Jill," Ramie yells. "Wait up."

The hallway fizzes with the usual crush of students, so I can reasonably fake not hearing her. I feel bad about it, but cut me some slack because I have a lot to deal with today, okay?

About ten feet from the Jed Barnsworthy vortex, Tommy appears, his face registering surprise at my new "haircut." Stopping at the intersection, he waits for me. I take a deep breath and try to psych myself up for acting nonchalant. When I reach him, he brushes his fingers down my arm.

"Hey, gorgeous," he says. He checks out the back and the sides. "I like it. It makes me want to kiss your neck." He pulls me close.

"Get a room," Jed Barnsworthy says.

The dirtbag holding up the wall next to him sniffs and says, "Yeah, get a gay room, you gayer."

Tommy ignores him. So do I. It gets easier to do this all the time.

I grab the back of my exposed neck. "What? You hate it."

Tommy shakes his head very slowly, then steps up to me and whispers in my ear, "You want to ditch school?"

I pull back. "Are you serious?"

"Come on," he says. "What are they gonna do? Expel us?

We can go to the beach and cram for calculus. It's the only class I'm worried about. And you? You're straight A's, right?"

I shrug.

Behind me, Jed and his toady boys giggle like hyenas. Then the shadow of Jed himself looms over me. Tommy pulls me away down the North Wing, but not soon enough. With a rough swipe, Jed whacks the back of my head. "Nice do," he says. There is a painful tug of hairpins and a sudden shadow over my right eye. But it's the shock on Tommy's face that confirms the worst. I reach up to center the wig just as Sammy Burston—one of Jed's toady boys—peels himself off the wall and lunges for me. In a swift and brutal motion, he yanks the wig clean off my head.

"Ow!" I scream. The breeze from an air-conditioning vent chills my head through the mesh skullcap.

"Holy shit!" Sammy snorts.

He tosses the wig in the air and it lands on the shoulder of some freshman girl, who squeals and brushes it off like a spider. Frantically, I try to cover my scabby head with one hand while lunging for the wig, but Sammy gets to it first.

"Yo, Barnsworthy," he says.

"Please," I whimper while trying to disappear completely.

Holding the wig behind his back, Sammy laughs, showing yellow teeth. "Barnsworthy," he says. "Check this out." He holds the wig above his head as I make pitiful and fruitless attempts to grab it.

I can hear the whispers and stunned exclamations of my

fellow students, but Jed stands stiffly, mouth opened. In place of mockery is something else, something far worse.

Finally, Tommy regains his senses, steps between me and Sammy Burston and says, "Hand it over, you little turd."

Sammy thrusts out his chin. "Make me, you homo." He searches out Jed Barnsworthy. But Jed's still looking at me, his eyes flicking between my face and my skullcap. The sneer has vanished. The smirk, the snark, the ever-present snide chuckle are all gone. In their place is the shadow of the Jed I used to know, the sad, shy, chubby Jed from the neighborhood, the Jed who made me promise not to tell anyone about Barbie Dress-up Treasure Hunt. I want to kill him.

Tommy lunges for the wig, but Sammy pulls it away.

That's when Ramie makes her appearance. Shoving her way through the knot of mute onlookers, she charges past Tommy and knees Sammy Burston in the nuts. Everyone gasps in unison.

Sammy gurgles painfully, then doubles over and releases the wig. Ramie snatches it, grabs my wrist and drags me to the girls' room around the corner. Stunned cries of "Oh my God!" and "Did you see her head?" trail us like flies until the heavy steel door banishes everything.

"The little monster," Ramie says. "Somebody owes that ass hat an ass kicking." She pulls me toward the big mirror above the sinks. Behind us, a tittering swarm of girls pushes the door open to peer in. Ramie hands me the wig, lunges at the door and slams it shut.

I try to put the wig on with shaky hands. Ramie stands with her back to the door, pressing it shut against the swarm outside. "Jill?" she says. "Hold on." She opens the door and shouts, "Get away from this door or you're all going to die." She slams it shut.

My fingers shake as I try to slide the wig on, but it keeps slipping down over my forehead.

"Jill?"

"Don't."

She walks over to me. "What happened to your hair?"

"Ramie," I say. "This is hard. I need to concentrate."

She hangs back for a few seconds while I struggle to position the wig before pulling it back over the skullcap. Then she leans against the sink next to me. "What's going on, Jill?"

I close my eyes and take a deep breath, hoping stupidly that she'll disappear. When I open them, she's looming over me with her big stupid hair and her bony shoulders stretching the fabric of her practically see-through Tinkerbell T-shirt. She pulls herself up to sit on the sink, her long fingers gripping the edge of it like talons. "Jill," she says. "What aren't you telling me?"

Ignoring her, I get the wig fixed over the front of my head and try to guide it back over the rest of my head.

"Here," Ramie says. She puts her hand on the front of the wig to help, but I yank my head away.

"Why do you keep doing that?" she says.

Holding the wig perched on the top of my head, I stare at her from a few feet away. She looks so confused, so scared.

"Is it . . ." She looks down. When she looks up again, there are tears in her eyes. "Is it chemo?"

I hold her gaze for a few seconds, then stare into the mirror and pull the wig all the way on.

"Jill?"

Chemo? Can I use this? Is this the lie I need to escape Ramie's mind probe?

"I've got to go," I say. Shouldering my backpack, I head to the door.

Ramie hops off the sink and follows me. "Where are you going?"

"I'm late," I say.

Whipping the door open, I rush down the mercifully empty hallway.

But I don't go to class. Instead, I sneak out through the goth door into the harsh bright sunlight of the parking lot. I stare at the pavement as I head to my car. The wig charade is over. Now I have to decide whether to go with the chemo story. Is it too depressing? Will I have to lose weight and wear pale makeup to sell it? Would that be offensive? I think it might be offensive to pretend you have cancer when all you have is a penis once a month.

When I get to my car, I spot Tommy leaning against the bumper.

"I had a feeling you'd run," he says.

I stop a safe distance from him, my backpack heavy on my shoulder. "Tommy—"

"I won't," he says. "Run, I mean."

I let my backpack drop with a thud. "Tommy, it's not chemo."

"Really?"

In the distance, by the Dumpsters, the goths laugh at something and stomp out their cigarettes.

"Really," I say.

He doesn't believe me.

"I have to get out of here," I say.

"Did you join the marines?" he says.

Is it possible to mock someone while still being incredibly sweet?

Yes.

"You still want to go to the beach?" I say.

He nods.

It's only a fifteen-minute drive down Argilla Road to Karn Beach, but the silence stretches it out. I can't figure out a way to disprove the hastily formed but apparently universally agreed upon "Chemo Theory" without blowing the lid off the even worse truth.

Karn Beach's huge parking lot, packed during summer vacation, is empty but for two cars parked on opposite corners. I pull up near the entrance to a little-known boardwalk that snakes into the dunes. Silently, we get out of the car and I retrieve a blanket, which has been in the trunk since last summer. There's a ketchup stain on one side of it and I can't remember which.

Tommy eyeballs the boardwalk entrance, which is partially obscured by an overhanging tree. "Isn't there supposed to be a psycho living back there somewhere?"

"Yup." I close the trunk. "And a nudist colony and the Karn Beach rapist and I think the Unabomber at one point. Scared?"

He laughs, then follows me under the tree.

The boardwalk creaks beneath us, and the overhanging trees create a welcome chill against the hot sun. When we emerge from the trees, the rolling dunes spread out in all directions, but only a sliver of ocean is visible in the valley between two of them.

"Wow," Tommy says. "I didn't know it was so big."

"Yeah." I take off my gold flats and step barefoot into the still-cool sand. "It stretches for miles, you know. Gets pretty hot back here in the summer."

"I bet." He steps out of his white Adidas and joins me barefoot in the sand. "Where to?"

"This way." I head off toward my favorite dune.

When we get there, I spread the blanket out and sit on one corner. The ocean is just visible over the top of another dune, and the rhythm of crashing waves reaches us. Tommy puts one shoe on each corner to secure the blanket, then sits next to me.

"So," he says.

I reach over him and pull his heavy backpack onto the blanket. Unzipping it, I pull out the calculus book.

"I hate math," he says. "Can't I just resign myself to not being a numbers person?"

"It's not about numbers." Sitting cross-legged, I open the book. "It's about nature."

"Nature?"

"Yeah."

He sits directly across from me, mirroring my cross-legged position. "All right. I'm listening."

The breeze unsettles the ends of my wig, and I keep checking to make sure it's secure. "All right, well, everything in this book is proof that all of this . . ." I gesture to the surrounding dunes. "That everything around us works the way it should."

He smiles suddenly, but the smile fades.

"It's a way of describing the natural order," I say, "and the relationships between things in an abstract way."

The smile won't return.

I close the book. "Go ahead," I say. "Ask me."

"So it's not from chemotherapy?" he says.

I stare at the cover of the book with its nerdy geometric drawing. "No. It's not."

He traces the blue line in the drawing on the book. "So how did it happen?"

I realize at this moment how reckless it was to rely solely on the integrity of the wig. I should have brainstormed a backup story.

Tommy's elbows rest on his knees as he leans forward, anxious for my answer.

Stalling, I lean back and drop onto the blanket. "I guess this is my fate."

Tommy hovers above me, his face blocking the sun. "What fate?"

"Always having to explain myself," I say.

Pulling myself up, I grab my sunglasses from the backpack and put them on.

Tommy lies on his side with his head propped on his hand. "Explain what?" he says.

I want to join him, to stretch myself out in his shadow, but I'm too scared.

"You know," I say. "This condition I have."

"The blood condition?" he says. "The transfusions?"

I turn my mirror shades to him. Feeling suddenly safe behind them, I fantasize for a nanosecond about spilling the whole truth. "Yeah," I say. "That. It sucks. It deeply sucks. And sometimes at the hospital . . ." I face the crest of a distant dune. "They make mistakes."

Tommy sits up. "Mistakes?"

I feel him studying me.

"Yeah." Now I can't look at him. Not when I'm lying like this.

"Are you telling me they cut off your hair by accident?"

It's only when *he* says it that I realize the full extent of its malness. But now I'm committed.

"Hard to believe," I say. "I know."

He scoots closer, takes my sunglasses off and places them on the blanket. "Jill," he says. "You can tell me anything. Or you can tell me nothing. But please don't lie to me."

When I breathe in, the jaggedness of it surprises me. I don't want to cry. I don't want to lose control and tell him the truth. He only thinks he wants it. He can't possibly want it. How could he?

"I'm sorry," I say.

Tommy wraps his long arms around me and pulls me to his

chest. “It’s okay,” he says. “You can tell me when you’re ready. I’ll wait.”

“Okay.” The word limps out as a few tears moisten his neck. Pulling back, I wipe his skin dry and try to stem the sniffling. “I’m sorry.”

He pulls me back to his shoulder and says, “Go ahead. Cry all you want. I’m not going anywhere.”

I let loose with a full-throated sob. “Thank you.”

He places his hand on the back of my wig and I hold my breath in embarrassment. Then he strokes it very gently. “It’s okay,” he says.

I wrap my arms around him and press as much of myself against his chest as I can manage. As soon as the well of tears dries up, he whispers as quietly as the breeze, “Jill.”

But it’s not a question. It’s just a word, a sound. Then his lips are on my neck. After a few gentle kisses, they wander to my cheek, my forehead. He pulls back just enough to focus on my eyes, and my body goes liquid.

Softly, our mouths connect. The sun appears and disappears behind the shadow of his face. He pulls himself impossibly close to me, our bodies growing hot against each other. I feel dizzy, like I’m falling. Then I realize he has been pushing me in the smallest of increments backward toward the blanket, his lips never leaving mine. With his hands firmly grasping the small of my back, he lays me down. Then slowly, gently, he lays his full length down on me. Our legs intertwined, he kisses me deeply. Our tongues connect. I feel pressure on the inside of my right knee. He’s pressing it. As his hands wander to my shoulders, then my face, the pressure grows until he's slid both of his legs between mine.

"Jill," he says.

I can't speak. My lips can only find his and kiss him deeper. Always deeper. I can feel him pressing against my pelvis. My knees bend and he positions himself lower, sending a warm ripple of pleasure through my torso.

His hand wanders across my shoulder to the top button of my shirt. The kiss grows harder. As I wrap my legs around his hips, he slips open the first button of my shirt, then the second, then the third. At the last button, he pulls his lips from mine, leans back and opens my shirt. His eyes flutter closed for a second. Then his face descends to my chest, over my bra and downward, his lips brushing the exposed skin of my ribs. Downward to the notch beneath my ribs, his lips find my stomach. He brushes them over the waistband of my jeans while fingering the front clasp of my bra. I don't know where to focus. He's touching me everywhere. After fumbling for a few seconds, he pops the clasp, looks up at me and pulls the bra open. An excited breath escapes his lips; then he pulls himself up and kisses my neck.

I clutch the back of his head as my eyes squeeze shut, the sun making pinwheels of color against my lids. "Tommy," I say. "Oh, Tommy."

I feel the wetness of his mouth on my neck as it slides lower. He's moving faster now, his hands never stopping as they stroke and caress my arms, my legs, my stomach. My thighs squeeze tightly around his hips as my hands wander up and down his back. When he moves his face downward over my ribs to the soft flesh of my stomach, my back arches and I feel my head dig into the yielding sand beneath the blanket.

Tommy sucks and bites at my stomach, then tugs at the snap of my jeans.

I gasp.

He looks up, eyes full of hope. His teeth come together in a knowing smile and he rips the snap open.

I freeze.

All feeling disappears.

Eyes glued to mine, Tommy grasps the zipper between his thumb and forefinger and, with an impossible slowness, pulls it downward. The sun burns my eyes, but I can't stop looking at him. As if challenging me to stop him, he stares back while pulling the zipper.

The sound of metal against metal is huge, all out of proportion. Everything but my own crotch and Tommy's hand on it disappears as the descending zipper reveals the pink cotton of my underwear.

"Wait." My hand clamps down on his.

The unzipping stops. He waits for my signal.

Everything's wrong.

His face. His hair.

My exposed breasts, the smooth hollow beneath my ribs. All wrong. Where's the fine trail of hair? Where's the bulge beneath my jeans where Tommy's face is?

And why is it Tommy's face? Why isn't it—

"Oh mal," I hear myself say.

Squirming out from under him, I pull my shirt closed. I don't even bother to reclasp my bra, which dangles gracelessly from my shoulders.

Tommy gets to his knees. "It's okay. We don't have to . . ."

I button my shirt as quickly as my fingers will manage.

"I'm sorry," he says. "I'm moving too fast."

I don't look at him as I battle with my zipper. I have to kneel to zip it.

"I'm sorry, Jill. I—"

"What?" I close the button of my jeans and glance around the dunes. No one is there.

"Are you okay?" he says.

The wind blows his hair so feebly.

"I mean, we don't have to, you know, if I'm moving too fast. It's cool."

It's anything but cool. My body's on fire with a devouring hunger that's all wrong. I want to run. I want to burrow into the dunes and disappear. Tommy's face—the faint hint of stubble, the severe jaw—is all wrong. Everything is wrong.

Saying nothing, we shake out the blanket and make our way back to the boardwalk and the parking lot.

I've freaked Tommy out. He has no idea what's going on. I know it's up to me to say something, but I'm so afraid of what I'm feeling right now, I can't speak.

I drive him back to school in utter, agonizing silence, watch him walk back inside, then drive home and go straight to my room.

Jack!

He's polluted my mind. All the disgusting things he does and thinks and dreams about have escaped his phase and are perverting mine!

But I won't have it. It's bad enough that he's driven a creepy wedge of uncomfortable pervitude between me and Ramie. He's not taking Tommy Knutson away from me too.

I put a note on the outside of my bedroom door telling Mom to leave me alone to meditate; then I do four and a half hours of it. I don't care how long I have to lie here conjuring the black dot. I am burying that little pervert in an unmarked grave.

When I get to school the next day, the Chemo Theory has become dogma. There's even talk of making me prom queen as a final tribute before I snuff it. The worst part is I can't refute the theory because I have no alternate.

In art class, I'm washing blue tempera paint out of a brush when Ramie comes in with the bell.

"Let's ditch," she says. "Want to hang out in Vietnam?"

Vietnam is a big obstacle course in the woods behind the visitor bleachers of the football field. For three weeks every year, Mr. Gibbons uses it to torture sophomores to build self-esteem. His or theirs, I've never been sure.

I shake out the brush and place it in the drying rack as the rest of the class gathers their stuff and vacates.

"Come on," Ramie says.

"I don't know, Rames."

I do not make eye contact, because despite all the meditation, I have not been able to evict the residue of Jack's icky wrong feelings. Undaunted, she presses her body right up to me and sticks her bony finger in my side. "You're coming with me, princess. This is a gun and I'm not afraid to use it."

"Very funny."

"Try me."

I squirm away from her, holding my breath against the coconut scent of her hair. "I've got study hall," I say. "I'm going to the library." I grab my backpack from the table under the pitying gaze of Mrs. Warren, who, like everyone else at Winterhead High, believes I am moments away from death.

Ramie charges around me and plants her ass on the table, gripping both of my wrists in her talonlike fingers. "Jill, please."

Mrs. Warren ambles over. "Come on, girls. You're going to be late."

Ramie hops off the table and clings to me as I head to the door. When we get to the hallway, she takes my wrist forcefully and charges me toward the band room.

"Ramie!"

"Shut up."

The band room is empty and, more importantly, features its own exterior door, which none of the instrument-playing goody-goodies ever exploits.

"Come on," she says.

She opens the door and yanks me outside. I don't resist anymore, because when Ramie gets to this level of conviction, there's no point. She takes my hand and we run across the football field and under the visitor bleachers to the woods. In a clearing, Mr. Gibbons's dreaded obstacle course hangs ominously from some trees.

"Yuck." I stare at the slats of wood nailed into a tree going up at least twenty feet. "I got halfway up that thing and panicked," I tell Ramie. "Mr. Gibbons was holding the rappelling harness or whatever it's called and he said he wouldn't catch me if I bailed out. He said I had to climb all the way to the top, ring that lame-ass bell and then jump. What a psycho."

Ramie lowers herself to a felled tree trunk. "Yeah," she says, "you know it's called Vietnam for a reason. Don't know the full story. He came back a changed man or something. Definitely a sadist, but you can't be too harsh on him."

I sit down on a tree stump. "I guess."

"So," she says. "Obviously you've been avoiding me because you don't want to talk about what happened to your hair."

"Ramie—"

"It's okay," she says. "I'm not going to ask again."

"Really?"

Ramie nods. "But I am going to ask about the bars on your window. What's that about?"

"Oh," I say. Then I try to think of something quick. "You know. Parents. Kind of paranoid. Crime and stuff."

"They're only on *your* window," she says.

I poke at the dirt and pebbles with the toe of my shoe. "Yeah, well, they started with my window. They're putting them up everywhere."

"Why?"

I shrug and consider drawing my weirdo father into the hastily improvised cover story. Conversely, I could blame my control-freak mother. But I haven't researched either of these lies and I am no good at improvised deception. "I don't know," I say. "Why do parents do any of the things they do?"

She stares at me and nods slowly. Then she leans back and looks up at the sky. "So I've been thinking."

"Hold on. Let me put on some safety gear."

She laughs. "About the prom."

"Yeah?" I pick up a twig and start peeling the bark off. "What about it?"

"I was thinking maybe we could go together."

"What?"

"Tommy's not going, right?"

"I haven't exactly given up on that yet, Rames."

"Yeah, but, you know. This is his first and last year at Winterhead High. The prom doesn't have any significance to him. But for us . . ."

"Since when does the prom have significance for you? I thought it was a stupid sexist tradition."

"No, Jill, homecoming court is a stupid sexist tradition. Prom is just stupid. At least I used to think that. Maybe I was wrong."

"I didn't think that was possible."

"Rare," she says, "but not impossible. Think about it." Her face brightens as she walks over and crouches in front of me. "We can style ourselves to the teeth. I mean whole hog. All out."

Visions of Ramie wrapping me in burlap and plastic sheeting dance in my head.

She puts her hands on my knees. "You never know. Might even make old Tommy jealous." She winks at me, then walks back to her felled tree and sits down.

"What about Mr. No-name?" I say.

Her face falls.

I'm stunned. Why would I bring up Jack at a moment like this? Why would I bring up Jack ever?

Ramie rests her elbows on her knees and studies the dirt. "You were right about him."

"I was?"

She stands up and paces in front of the log. "Yeah, I guess I can check One-Night Stand with Peeping Tom off my list of things to do."

"Ramie," I say. "I'm really sorry it turned out like that. You know you deserve better. He's a jerk."

She shrugs and kicks at the log. I wonder if Jack realizes how much he's hurt her with his little stunt. He should have known we'd put an end to it. He was reckless and stupid and now Ramie's paying the price. What a selfish jerk.

Between my feet, a black beetle emerges from behind a thick blade of grass. I position my gold flat above it, then decide at the last minute to spare its life. When I look up, Ramie is climbing the slats of the twenty-foot tree.

"Uh, Rames." I get up and stand underneath her, my head level with her ankles. "What are you doing?"

"Climbing."

"Well, stop it. Climbing down is much harder than climbing up. That's how Mr. Gibbons made it so you'd have to jump."

She keeps going, getting smaller and smaller as she rises.

"Ramie, stop it!" I step on the first slat and start to make my way up. But I only get about five feet off the ground when I realize that first, I'm too scared to go any higher, and second, I can't exactly carry Ramie down on my shoulders. I feel for the lower slat with the toe of my gold flat and slowly, awkwardly make my way down.

Ramie keeps going. "Hey, you can see Daria's house from up here."

"Ramie, get down."

"Why should I?"

I take a few steps back. Her long dark form looks so small against the green sun-dappled canopy. "What is wrong with you?" I say. "Do you know how dangerous that is?"

Hugging the tree with both arms, she climbs higher.

"Ramie!"

"Wow!" she says. "This is really high."

"Ramie, you're going to fall! Is that what you want? Is this some cry for attention?"

"Hah!" Her black boot finds another slat, but when she presses her foot to it, it slips off.

"Ramie!"

She slides down over three slats but stops herself by hugging the tree. I turn away and wait for the thud, but when I look up, she's climbing again.

"Ramie, stop it right now!"

She places one foot on either side of a large slat of wood and loosens her grip on the tree. "So," she says. "My woman of mystery." She inches her torso away from the tree.

"What are you doing!"

She pushes herself farther out. "You think *this* is a cry for attention?"

"What?"

"You think I *like* making my friends worry about me?"

"Ramie, please don't do this. I'll tell you everything. I promise."

Clinging to the tree with both arms, Ramie lifts one foot off the slat and swings her leg out.

"Ramie!"

Her big silver belt buckle glistens in the sun.

"I'm sorry," I say. "I'm so sorry. Please just stay put and let me get Mr. Gibbons."

"It's too late for that," she says. Then, in one breathless moment, she pushes herself off the tree, leaving a horrifying gap between it and her falling body.

My feet carry me forward to catch her, but her body does a strange thing. It stops falling downward and starts falling sideways, past the tree and over my head. Dumbfounded, I watch her fly across the clearing.

It wasn't a big silver belt buckle. Ramie wasn't wearing a belt.

"Kowabunga!" she screams as the now-visible rappelling rope carries her to a pile of sand at the edge of the clearing.

With her legs hinged out in front of her, she lands with a thud and collapses in a heap on the sandpile.

I run to her, tripping over the tree stump.

"Ramie!"

When I get to the pile of sand, she rolls over and disconnects herself from the rope.

"I could kill you," I say.

"Sucks, doesn't it?"

"You went up there without a safety rope."

She shrugs, still lying in the sand.

"You could have fallen."

"I know."

She sits up and I drop to my knees in front of her.

"Why?" I say.

There are tears in her eyes.

"Why!" I say.

"I love you," she says. "I'm supposed to be your best friend and you're not telling me something so important it scares you." She wipes her nose across the back of her hand. "If you think you're sparing me, trust me, you're not. I'm in hell I'm so worried about you. I don't know if you're sick or if your mother is locking you up and performing lobotomies on you." She wipes her nose with the back of her arm, then dabs at her eyes with her knuckles. "Why won't you talk to me?"

Still on my knees, I move closer to her. "Ramie, I . . ."

She sits up fully now, her face only inches from mine. "Tell me, Jill. *Please.*"

In the distance, Mr. Gibbons blows his whistle twice.

"Tell me," she says.

There is so much hunger in Ramie's eyes. So much fear. She takes my hand and interlaces her fingers with mine. "Tell me."

The smell of coconut drifts up from her hair. "Please," she says.

Her lips part, her white teeth just visible.

"I . . ."

"It's okay," she says. "Whatever it is, we can get through it together."

Her red lips curl and stretch around the words.

"I . . ."

"Just say it, Jill."

"But I . . ."

"You know I love you, no matter what."

"Oh, Ramie." I lean in and press my lips to hers.

For a brief moment, we connect, the warm fullness of her lips squishing against mine.

Then Ramie pulls away. Eyes wide, her body stiffens. "Oh." Her face softens as she runs her hand down my arm. "Jill, I didn't know. I mean . . ."

Leaning back on my heels, I rise to a standing position. The woods blur and sway. I keep my feet wide to steady myself. Faintly, I hear Ramie's voice, but I don't know what she's saying. Turning my back to her, I walk through the clearing.

I think she follows me, but I can barely sense anything except the hard-packed dirt at my feet. Then something else impresses itself on my narrowed vision.

Tommy Knutson.

He stands at the edge of the clearing, openmouthed.

I pass him without a word, without even meeting his eyes. I cross in front of the bleachers, then walk right past the soccer field, where Mr. Gibbons hands out quivers and bows for archery lessons.

I think he says "Miss McTeague," but I don't stop. I do notice his attention turn to something behind me, presumably Ramie and/or Tommy. I focus my attention on putting one foot in front of the other, getting all the way to the band room door before I realize I've left my backpack in the clearing.

The rushed patter of footsteps in the grass gathers behind me, then stops.

"Jill?" Tommy says.

"You don't have to run," Ramie says.

I keep my back to them. "Ramie," I say. "Did you, by any chance, pick up my backpack?"

"Yeah, it's right here," she says.

I reach back blindly, grab it and run for the parking lot.

Both of them call after me, but mercifully, they do not follow.

As I'm driving home, my cell phone never stops ringing. While I'm waiting at a red light, I listen to the succession of messages they've left. The first one is from Ramie, telling me how unbelievably okay she is with my feelings for her. She didn't mean to make me feel mal or anything. The second one is from Tommy, who apologizes for spying on me in the clearing. He's worried, just like Ramie. I shouldn't feel bad about kissing Ramie, though. There's nothing wrong with it. If that's why I cut off all my hair, I should know that that's okay too. He has a cousin who used to cut herself. She got therapy, though, and seems to be all right now. The third message is from Ramie, who tells me I'm not alone, no matter how much it feels that way.

But Ramie doesn't know what alone is.

When I get home, I run up the front steps and close the door on the outside world for good.

When Mom comes home, I tell her everything and she agrees with my assessment that I can never, under any circumstances, return to Winterhead High. Ever. Somehow she has to figure out a way for me to take my final exams at home.

The next day, she makes some phone calls from her office and the job is done. My days at Winterhead High are over. I spend the rest of my phase at home, not answering my cell phone and hiding when Tommy or Ramie—or both of them together—come over to try to convince my dad to let them in. Dad is surprisingly good at sympathizing with their concerns without ever wavering in his refusal to let them in. I told him I'd kill myself if he wavered.

When the workers come to install the new Jack-proof security system in my room, I move my things into the TV room. It's not easy filling up whole days without school. We don't have the Internet, so I spend a lot of time watching daytime TV, which is unbelievably depressing. I have to endure way too frequent visits from Dad, who thinks it's his new mission in life to emerge from the yoga hole to have one-sided heart-to-hearts with me.

One day, while I'm watching some hostage situation unfold

on CNN, he comes up, shirtless and stinking of BO, with two jam jars full of jasmine tea.

"Hey, kiddo," he says. He hands me an unasked-for jam jar, sits on the far corner of the leather sectional and nods benignly at me. "Cabin fever yet?"

"Huh?"

He presses his sweaty back into the beige leather and has a sip of his tea.

I hate jasmine tea, but it's not worth starting a conversation with him over it.

"Just curious, Jilly-girl. How long do you plan to keep this up?"

A loud rug-cleaning commercial comes on the TV and I mute it.

"Keep what up?"

"Hiding out like this," he says. "Look, sweetie, take it from me, it's not an easy life."

"Dad, please. I don't have a choice here. Jack has destroyed my life at Winterhead High. He's destroyed my life, period."

"How has he done that, sweetheart? By cutting off your hair?"

I have a sip of the unsweetened tea. Dad doesn't believe in refined sugars. Dad doesn't believe in anything but tofu, quinoa and jasmine tea.

"No, Dad. It's a lot more than that. He's . . . I don't even know how to explain it."

"Well," he says. "I've got plenty of time. Give it a try."

Right. Because advice from the mentally ill is bound to be useful.

"Look, Dad, I know you're trying to help, but—"

"But you don't want my help. You want to curl up and disappear. I get that."

"Yeah, sure. You get it."

"Honey?"

"You couldn't possibly get it, Dad. Jack hasn't just snuck out of the bedroom. He's snuck out of his phase. I don't know how he's done it but he's all over my brain. Plan B isn't working anymore. He's injected himself into my life, into my . . ."

I put the jam jar of tea on the glass coffee table and unmute the TV. We both turn our attention to the tediously unfolding hostage situation.

"Synthesis," Dad says.

"What?"

He stands up and stares through the sliding glass door. The neglected wooden deck is warped and cracked, but he's not looking at that. He's looking past that, to the woods at the edge of our backyard. "Just something to consider, sweetheart."

He takes his tea and his oniony aroma back down into the yoga hole.

On the TV, a dark blob appears in one of the lower windows of the office building.

Synthesis. Sure, Dad. I'll Google it right away.

Mom and Dad disagree on the security system. For one thing, it's costing a fortune. For another, Dad thinks tightening the locks on Jack's prison will only worsen the situation. I've decided not to form an opinion on the subject. I've outsourced the decision to Mom. My time is spent trying to banish Jack down into the yoga hole of my own mind. It's not that I'm remembering the things he does. Those memories are still buried. It's the creepy desires and deviant longings I can't seem to suppress.

The only peace I get anymore is from the black dot. But as soon as I open my eyes, the feelings return. Plus I can't stop thinking about Ramie and the clearing, about the millisecond between our lips meeting and Ramie pulling away. I think about it, feel sick, try to banish it. But my mind keeps wandering back to it. It's Jack. I know it is. He's trying to fix the memory so he can replay it over and over. He's a memory thief. And now he's manipulating me to enact the memories he wants in store. He wants more Ramie and less Tommy. That has to be it. He *made* me kiss Ramie. There's no other way to explain it.

JUNE 20

Jack

At first, I'm not even sure I'm awake. I think my eyes are open, but it's so dark I can't see. When I roll over to reach for the clock on the table, neither the clock nor the table is there.

"What the . . ."

My voice echoes. Sitting up, I swing my legs to the edge of the bed. My feet hit the floor before they should, bending my knees into an awkward angle. I wait for my eyes to adjust, but there's nothing to adjust to.

Standing, I stick my hands out and walk like Frankenstein to the light switch by the door. My hands scrape the rough wall but find no light switch.

The place reeks of fresh paint.

I slide my hands up and down the wall next to the doorjamb, but it's smooth. The smell of paint is unbearable. I grab the doorknob and pull. It's locked, of course. Just beneath the doorknob is a rectangular hunk of metal. Running my fingers over it, I hear a quiet bip. Then a green dotted line lights up in a display panel, casting just enough light to reveal a number pad below. I drop to my knees and examine it. It's a security system. Standing, I back up and let my eyes adjust to the faint light from the panel, then take in the room. The only shape I can make out is the vague blob of my bed. To my right, a dark rectangle signals what I think is the bathroom. As I walk to it, my feet step reassuringly from carpet to cold tile. When I reach for the light switch by the door, my hand finds something new. I try to flick it up, but it's one of those sliding controls. I slide it up and am instantly blinded by a sickening fluorescent glow.

When my eyes adjust, I realize that the room is the same shape as my bathroom, but everything's missing. The shower curtain, the mirror, the shelves, the vanity, the refrigerator. It's all gone.

I back out into the bedroom.

It too is the right shape, the right proportions, but in the dim light spilling from the bathroom, all I recognize is my bed. No, on closer inspection, I realize it's not my bed. It's a new one. No box spring. No frame. Just a thick mattress on the floor. A stack of white T-shirts and boxer briefs sits where the closet used to be, and lying in front of them is the last outfit Jill wore—a black and white striped T-shirt, a pair of orange sweatpants and a pink thong.

My eyes wander to the space where the wooden chest used to sit, then upward to the metal plates where the windows were.

Fists flying, I stumble to the door. "Let me out!"

I slam the meat of my balled fists into the unyielding steel, then drop to my knees and stare at the number pad. Closing my eyes, I summon the black dot, then snake into the rabbit hole of Jillspace in search of the code. It's not there. They'd never be that sloppy.

Muffled footsteps approach; then a metal slit opens at the bottom of the door. A brown cardboard tray slides through and drops to the carpet. On it are a peanut butter sandwich and a juice box. I crouch on the floor and peer through, catching a glimpse of my mother's beige pant leg before the slit slams shut. Jumping to my feet, I step on the sandwich and pound on the door.

"Let me out!"

When I stop and listen, I hear nothing, not even the sound of her leaving. I kick the cardboard tray aside and slide down the door. On my heel is a smear of peanut butter.

Chunky.

I kick the juice box across the room. What am I, three? Are they going to feed me Cheerios from a Ziploc bag too?

Then it occurs to me. Only flat things will fit through the slit. They don't intend to open this door. Ever. Not even to feed me. I lean my head against the door, defeated.

That's when I notice the dome.

In the center of the ceiling, surrounded by a steel grid, a mirrored dome hangs. I get to my feet for a closer look. Circling beneath it, I find no detail other than a smooth surface reflecting a warped image of my naked body. The sweat on the back of my neck suddenly chills.

It's a camera.

They're watching me.

I stumble backward into the bathroom and slam the door shut.

On the stainless steel sink are a stack of paper cups, a miniature toothbrush and a tube of Colgate. No floss. In the shower is a bottle of conditioning shampoo. Hung over the side of the tub is one towel.

I lift the toilet seat for a long piss, vowing to remain in the bathroom for the duration of my phase. Dick in hand, I look up to the ceiling for reassurance of privacy. Directly above my head is another, smaller dome.

Everything inside of me freezes. I can't piss. I can't even let go of my dick. There is no escape from their spying eyes. They've removed the closet. I can't crawl under the bed. I can't even hide behind the shower curtain. Everything I do is on display. Even pissing.

Closing the lid, I drop to the toilet seat and cover my face with my hands. As my shoulders shudder, I will myself not to cry. My legs bounce beneath me as the cold from the floor seeps through the soles of my feet. The only thing they've left is the slow and steady drip from the shower, which echoes fiercely now against the bare tile walls.

No hope. No future. No hand.

Just the painful need to urinate.

I stand up and take that long piss.

"Hi, Mom and Dad," I tell the mirrored face of their spy camera. "I'll be masturbating in here later on. Shall we say tenish?"

As I empty myself out, my mind churns through a host of

options—all of them fruitless, all of them strictly for entertainment value. I could piss on the rug. I could scratch myself raw, then bleed obscenities on the fresh white paint. I could scar my face with the soft miniature toothbrush or the edge of the toothpaste tube. I could bang my head against the wall until I give myself a concussion.

I stalk to the sink to splash cold water on my face. I'm about to brush my teeth when I decide to skip it. Let Jill wake up with yellow teeth, the traitor. Leaning against the steel sink, I stare up at the smooth semidome and wonder which one of them is watching me right now. I hope it's Mom. I hope she's blushing while looking at me naked, staring back at her. I won't get dressed. I'll walk around naked all day.

But it won't be Mom. Mom has a job. Someone has to pay for this high-tech experiment in sadism. It'll be Dad watching me most of the day. It'll be Dad on suicide watch.

The hard edge of the metal sink digs into my butt, but I don't move. I keep staring at my warped reflection in the semidome.

I could take him. All I'd have to do is find something to cut my wrists. When he comes in to rescue me, I can use the element of surprise to overtake him.

But they'll have thought of that, won't they? They'll have a box of tranquilizers by the door. I close my eyes and meditate my way through the black dot into Jillspace. Mom did mention tranquilizers to Jill, but when Jill protested, Mom promised to skip it. Then again, Mom's smart. She probably lied to

Jill to keep the information safe from me. You can't play hardball with Mom. If I act up and don't escape, she could have me tranqued up and in a straitjacket for the duration of my phase. Even Jill knew that.

I open the bathroom door and walk to the number pad again. Dropping to the floor, I sit naked on the scratchy carpet and wait for an idea to emerge. But to forge a plan, to even entertain the dream of escape, I need something to work with. What do I have?

Nothing. This is it for me. No matter what happens to Jill in the future, no matter what kind of freedom she eventually forges for herself, I'm finished.

I put my back to the door and slowly bang the back of my skull against it.

They've won. The four walls of this room are my universe now. I will never see sunshine. I will never see Ramie.

Acceptance does not sand the edges off this brutal reality. Nor does it shrink the scope of its awfulness. If anything, it feeds it, enlarges it until it's so huge and terrifying I can't find room for it in my puny brain.

I drag myself back to bed and hide under the covers, the only place their cameras don't reach.

Sleep doesn't come.

Three times a day, a brown cardboard tray appears through the slit. Three times a day, a sandwich and a juice box. They don't trust me with silverware and they don't want to create dirty dishes. They don't want any reason to have to open that door. I am hermetically sealed. The only way out is down the drain.

Sometimes I'm asleep. Sometimes I'm awake. I don't know if these cycles correspond with the sun and moon. I keep vague time based on the appearance of cardboard trays. Sometimes I daydream about a time in the future when Mom and Dad are dead, when there's no one left to guard this prison. Will I be free then? Can I live that long? Do I want to?

I can't even masturbate now. It's not the camera. As time passes, rage dissipates to low-grade resentment. Occasionally, I console myself with the fact that they have to spend all day watching me slouch, sleep, scratch my balls and relieve myself. It's a limp victory, but it's something.

When I think about Ramie, the fire of lust flickers, then fades as despair takes over. I can't do anything with that despair. I can't fashion it into a weapon or use it to manipulate my way out of this prison. What am I going to do? Cry my eyes out? Make pleading gestures to the camera? It's too late for that. My watchers have abandoned any sense of responsibility toward me. I'm not their son anymore. Truthfully, I never was.

Outside this prison, the world is rolling on. Winterhead High is preparing for the senior prom. Tommy Knutson is wondering what happened to his formerly normal girlfriend. Ramie is getting over me, writing me off as a Peeping Tom. That's how it will be until I am utterly forgotten.

I don't want you to think I've made peace with this. I haven't. But after a while, the self-pity starts to fatigue me and

I decide to fake a Zenlike state of acceptance, just to change things up a bit.

Not knowing what a person in a Zenlike state of acceptance would actually do, I start small. I take a shower and brush my teeth. Don't laugh. It's more than I've done all this phase. At the very least, it leaves me feeling physically different from the moping, stank-breath loser I've been since I woke up.

Then I lie down and start mining Jill's last day. No treasure trove of joy there, I can tell you. For some reason, Dad emerged from his om hole to read *Yoga Journal* in the TV room while Jill and Mom watched reruns of *Sex and the City.* Jill kept sneaking looks at him and wishing he'd leave because it's "mal" enough watching four New York City sluts discuss orgasms in front of your mom. In front of your dad, it's just gross. But Dad sat there on the maroon leather recliner, legs in the lotus position, eyes on his magazine. Every once in a while, he'd turn a page, look over at Jill and smile.

Wondering why he'd leave his yoga hole to watch a TV show he couldn't possibly appreciate, I replay the memory.

Dad didn't say anything. He just sat there silently reading his magazine through two episodes, then retreated to the basement. Mom shrugged when he did this, clinked the ice cubes in her glass of Diet Coke and had a sip.

Stop. Rewind.

I go back to a particular moment. On the TV, Charlotte was crinkling her nose at something Samantha said while the girls had brunch at that diner. Dad turned the page with a loud snap, which drew Jill's attention. Catching her eye over the top of his magazine, Dad darted his eyes downward for a second, then darted them back up to Jill.

Having no idea what he meant by this eyeball semaphore, Jill turned her attention back to the TV screen.

But something stuck.

I replay it again. I go back to the moment just after Dad's eyes darted downward. It was such a sudden move. Dad never makes sudden moves. He moves as if he's in water, everything slow and methodical.

Jill followed his eyes downward to the carpet and back up, past the magazine cover to Dad's face. His eyes flashed wide for just a second before he resumed reading.

But there was nothing on the carpet and nothing on the coffee table between them, except for a cinnamon-scented candle and an empty water glass.

Stop, rewind.

What else was on that coffee table? A coaster with blue and green ducks on it, a nail file and a crumpled paper towel bunched around an apple core.

So?

Dad was signaling something to Jill. Something he didn't want Mom to see.

Stop, rewind.

Back to the floor. But there was nothing on the floor. The carpet was spotless, a blank beige slate. Mom doesn't let anything accumulate in any room of the house.

I replay Jill's memory of glancing up from the coffee table, across the cover of *Yoga Journal,* where a skinny blond chick held a perfect Warrior One pose on a rocky beach with the surf crashing behind her. Big yellow letters against the blue of the sky announced "Sex and Yoga." At the bottom right-hand corner was the address label in print too small to read. Above that were some numbers Dad had scribbled in his jagged penmanship—a phone number, probably.

I follow Jill's gaze upward to Dad's face.

Wait a minute.

A phone number has ten digits.

Stop, rewind.

Back to the magazine cover, to the numbers above the address label. They were in red ink against the blue of the ocean. Seven, nine, three.

My pulse races.

There were more numbers than that. Breathing deeply, I sharpen the image.

Two.

Seven, nine, three, *something,* two.

A number is missing. A number that looks like a letter.

The letter S.

Five!

That's it. Seven, nine, three, five, two!

Dad wrote seven, nine, three, five, two on the cover of *Yoga Journal* and led Jill's eyes to it. Why?

My eyes pop open and I sit upright in bed. Then I throw the covers off and stumble to the door.

I'm about to enter the code when I stop myself. What time is it? Is anyone watching me? I turn off the light so that I am plunged in darkness. Then I press my ear to the door. I don't hear anything. But then, I haven't heard anything since I woke up. Do I act now or wait? I've lost track of time. I don't know how much remains of my phase.

And maybe I'm wrong. Maybe this is a trick. Maybe Dad was playing the lottery with those numbers. Why would he do it? Why would he tell Jill the code?

Screw it. I punch in the numbers one at a time and wait. A high-pitched beep slices the quiet, followed by the sound of metal on metal. Reaching up with a sweaty palm, I turn the doorknob.

It gives!

Pulling slowly, I open the door to the pitch-black hallway.

It's nighttime. And I'm still naked. I throw on some underwear and a T-shirt, then pull on Jill's orange sweatpants. They're low riding and way too short. They make me look like a jailhouse mime, but it's either that or Captain Underpants, so I decide to go with it. Shoeless, I creep out into the hallway and close the door with maximum gentleness. I toe-heel down the hallway, then the stairs, freezing at every creak. When I get downstairs, I stare at Mom's closed bedroom door. Part of me wants to sneak in and smother the bitch with her own pillow. The other part—the sensible part—wants to get the hell out of here before anyone knows what I'm up to.

On the kitchen wall by the sink is a clock that reads 2:37. That gives me a good four hours before Mom wakes up and realizes what's happened.

I creep into the vestibule, my bare feet sticking to the cold tiles. The door to Dad's basement yoga hole is closed. I want to go down there and thank him for freeing me. I want to ask him why he did it. And why he did it in such a cryptic, back-handed way. But the clock is ticking. I tug the screen door open, flip the lock on the front door and slip outside.

And once again, ladies and gentleman, the Jackmonster is free.

In my mime gear and bare feet, I run to the shed out back and disentangle Jill's ten-speed from between the two broken lawn mowers. The metal-toothed pedals dig into my bare feet, but I don't care. Leaving the shed door open, I mount the bike and hightail it to Main Street.

The road speeds by beneath my wheels as I race through sleepy Winterhead. Without slowing down, I veer left onto Cherry Street and sprint beneath the giant oak trees to Ramie's house.

I ride right up the gravel driveway and dump the bike in some bushes around the side of the porch. Then I shinny up the tree and pull myself to the porch roof. I'm about to knock on her window when I stop.

What do I tell her?

She thinks I'm a Peeping Tom. I *am* a Peeping Tom. Plus I haven't called or visited in two months and now I'm lurking outside her window in Jill's sweatpants. Will she recognize them? Is there a lie in the universe that can smooth over this bag of triangles?

I press my forehead to the window. Ramie sleeps curled on her side, facing me, with her mouth open.

I shiver in the cool night air as goose bumps break out over my exposed skin. Maybe the time for lying is over. Lying is what got me into this mess in the first place. Lying, scheming, plotting. All of it in service of Jill's conformist delusions.

Ramie's body rises and falls with her breathing. We've been lying to her for too long. Whatever rationalizations we've manufactured about the cruel world and its presumed inability to accept us, in the end, we've been lying to our best friend, the one person who *would* accept us. It's time to tell her the truth. All of it.

Hmm. I guess that's what they call a moment of clarity.

I bring my knuckles to the window and tap.

Ramie opens her eyes with a start. She breathes in sharply and looks confused and scared; then slowly, recognition dawns.

I wave meekly and mouth the word "hi."

Sitting up, she pulls the comforter around her bare shoulders, exposing the rest of her body. She's wearing old green gym shorts and a white tank top. I know that tank top. You can see her nipples through it. Not now, though. It's too dark. Her bare feet dangle from the bed as she perches on the edge, regarding me with skepticism. I try an apologetic smile, then press my palm against her window.

She twists her head over her shoulder to look at the doorway, then gets up and comes to the window, dragging the thick comforter like a wedding train. But she doesn't open the window.

I mouth the words "I'm sorry."

This makes her brow furrow and the skin just above her

nose wrinkle. Ramie's not one of those girls who looks cute when she's mad. When she's mad, she looks mad. Fierce, even. When Jill once accused her of flirting with Emerson Bilmont, on whom Jill had a ferocious and thoroughly ignored crush, Ramie launched an expression missile of such menace that the UN would have classified it as a weapon of mass destruction.

This look is different. She's trying to be angry, but in her eyes, her true feeling is plain. She wants me. She's going to open the window. She just wants me to suffer first. I'm suffering plenty. As I press my palm against the glass and allow her dark brown eyes to swallow me, I am suffering against the tick-tock of the clock of doom. Plus I'm on the verge of bursting through my underwear *and* Jill's sweatpants.

Just as I think this, Ramie's eyes wander downward and register surprise at my unusual dress.

I open my hands and form a nervous smile.

Ramie takes a visible deep breath just to show me how on the fence she is about letting me in. Then she places her long fingers in the notches and lifts the window. She steps aside and I slide in.

She stands stiffly by the bed, keeping the window open, as if to imply that my invitation is provisional.

"Your hair," she says.

How I've longed to hear that voice again with my own ears.

"You cut it," she says.

I shrug. "It was bugging me."

Her eyes wander downward to the orange sweatpants

again. "What are you wearing?" She looks up at me. "Are those—"

"My sister's," I say.

The comforter slips from her left shoulder and she shrugs back into it.

I take a step toward her and she pulls her head back.

"I don't have a lot of time," I say. "I can never go back."

"Back where?"

"Home."

Suspicion melts to concern. "Why?" she says.

I sit on the edge of her bed, which is still warm. "Ramie," I say. "I have to tell you something."

"First," she says, "tell me your name."

"It's Jack."

"Jack what?"

I look at her, silhouetted against the window. How I've longed to see her without the veil of memory between us.

"Will you sit next to me?" I say.

She shakes her head.

"Ramie, listen, I know Jill told you I was probably a delinquent, but—"

"How do you know Jill?"

I look at the floor in search of the courage to continue. "Ramie, I'm not a delinquent. I'm—"

"What?" She steps forward, nudging my kneecaps with the edges of the comforter. "What are you?" She holds the comforter clasped in one slender hand, but its opening spreads to a wide V at her stomach, revealing her hip bones through the dark green gym shorts. "And how do you know Jill?"

I bring my hands to the V and grip the edges of the comforter. A deep breath rises from her diaphragm as I spread the comforter open and crest it over her shoulders. Pulling it taut against the small of her back, I spread my legs and pull her toward me. "Don't you know?" I say.

Our legs lock together like LEGOs. She leans back to look down at me, her eyes searching my face, my head, my neck. She touches the uneven outcroppings of hair, then runs her long fingers down my cheek. When her finger finds the scar under my chin, she stops breathing.

"I can never go back," I say. "I'm—"

She falls to me, her soft lips finding mine. The comforter falls in a heap to the floor and I wrap my arms around her waist. Lifting her up, I slide backward onto the bed. The hot skin of her stomach through the flimsy tank top presses against me, and I inch back further until we are lengthened across the bed, every possible inch of my arms, torso and thighs pressed against every inch of hers.

With a gentle tug, she pulls her lips from mine and draws them across my cheek, then downward to my neck. "Jack," she says.

That's when I know that the truth, in all of its grotesque scientific detail, will have to wait. Her lips wander to my shoulder as she slides her body downward. There is another, more essential truth that requires its airing tonight. A truth that resides in the body. The truth of Ramie's warm skin. The way it smells. The truth of her legs wrapped around mine, the shocking revelation of her gym shorts in my grip, sliding downward over the taut skin between her hip bones. The smooth white truth of her breasts as I peel off her tank top. The sound of her startled breath as she frees me from my underwear.

It is more truth than words could ever hold. A truth that requires not one, not two, but three full airings before it has had its say. And when it is freed, it hovers moist and warm in the close, dark air of Ramie's bedroom while its human agents entwine.

And that *other* truth? What a small thing it is. What a trifle. Good night, ladies and gentlemen. Good night.

If ever there was a morning I wanted to last forever, it was that morning. Waking up with Ramie's big nest of black hair piled on my shoulder, her long arm thrown across my chest, her warm thigh on top of my own and the thrilling scratch of her—

There is a knock at the door.

"Ramie?" someone says. "Wake up, honey."

It's Ramie's mother.

"Jill's mom's here," she says.

In the frantic pause between those words and the turn of the doorknob, I slide from under Ramie's breathtaking weight. She moans softly but doesn't rouse. The door cracks open, revealing the shape of Ramie's mother as I drop to the floor in a crouch. Flattening myself against the cold wood floor, I peer out between the brass feet of Ramie's bed as her mother opens the door all the way and steps inside.

Above me, Ramie stirs in a whisper of sheets.

Mrs. Boulieaux's legs move toward the bed but stay mercifully on the other side of it, a mere three feet from me. All she'd have to do is glance over the other side to see me in all my naked glory. "Wake up, honey," she says.

Sheets rustle as Ramie scrambles to cover herself with the comforter. My underwear and orange sweatpants sit in a ball at the foot of the bed.

"Mrs. McTeague is downstairs," Mrs. Boulieaux says. "She says Jill is missing."

"What?" Ramie says.

The mattress sags with Mrs. Boulieaux's weight. "Honey," she says. "Where are your pajamas? Did you sleep naked last night?"

"Huh?" Ramie says. "Um, yeah. I got hot. Did you say Jill's missing?"

Mrs. Boulieaux gets up from the bed and her feet and legs move to the door. "Get dressed and come downstairs," she says. "Mrs. McTeague is waiting. She looks worried."

Mrs. Boulieaux leaves and shuts the door behind her. I see Ramie's naked legs and feet hit the floor on the other side of the bed. "Jack?" she whispers.

"I'm under the bed."

Her naked body drops into a crouch as she peers under the bed.

"She didn't see me," I say. "I made it in time. I think."

She stares at me through the dark, dusty space under the bed, her breasts crushed against her bent legs. I want to crawl across the dust bunnies and make love to her again.

Ramie brings her knees together protectively and covers her breasts with her arms. "I have to . . . um . . . Jill's . . . I have to—"

"Go downstairs," I say. "I heard. I'll sneak out the window."

I get to my feet and grab my underwear, painfully aware of her averted gaze. I slide into them and pull on the orange sweatpants and my T-shirt.

Dragging the thick comforter with her for protection, Ramie finds her gym shorts and slides into them, but our eyes meet before she can locate her tank top. Her arm twitches, but she resists covering her breasts. I turn away to give her some privacy as she hunts for the shirt. Through the window, I spot Mom's beige Saab in the driveway.

Ramie finds her tank top under a pillow and I struggle for something else to look at while she slides it down over her smooth vanilla torso. My eye catches on something pink and black dangling from the rack next to the vintage trench coats. "Is that a prom dress?" Next to it is a white tuxedo. "Are you going to the prom?"

Mrs. Boulieaux's voice calls up, "Ramie!" Then her footsteps climb the stairs.

I go to the window and open it. "Who's the tux for?"

"Ramie!" Mrs. Boulieaux calls, her footsteps approaching.

I lift the window and slide out into the cold. Pressing my body against the slim fringe of wood next to the window, I watch Ramie's mother open the door and urge Ramie out. Ramie looks back once in search of me, then follows her mother out the door.

I shinny down the maple tree and run barefoot across the stick-strewn lawn. I can only guess at the nightmare visions with which Mom is filling Ramie's head. Undoubtedly she is telling Ramie that a mutant swamp creature named Jack has swallowed Jill alive or that a top-secret military experiment has gone awry, unloosing a maniacal masturbator/girlkiller on Winterhead and its environs.

Digging my bike out of the bushes, I mount it and race across her lawn to Cherry Street.

I don't know what day it is or how much time I have left. Nor do I have any idea where to go. Turning the pedals as fast as I can, I head to Main Street.

I'm speeding past the Brownsteins' big yellow house when all of a sudden, my legs give out on me. Pulling over into the sandy shoulder, I drop the bike onto its side.

Holy crap! I had sex with Ramie last night!

I have to squat over my bike as the magnitude of this washes through me.

Ramie.

Me.

Naked.

A white SUV cruises down Cherry Street and slows as it

nears me. A middle-aged guy in a nylon tracksuit brings it to a stop, lowers the window and leans across the passenger seat. "You all right there?" he says.

Classic rock plays quietly on his radio.

"Huh?" I say.

"Are you hurt?" he says. "You fall off your bike?"

"Oh." I pick the bike up, but my knees are still wobbly. "No, I'm fine." *I've just deflowered your neighbor* is what I think but don't say out loud.

"You sure?"

"Yup." I straddle the bike. "Thanks for asking, though."

He waits as I mount the bike and wobble forward. Then he passes me slowly with a little wave. We both arrive at the intersection to Main Street at the same time and stare awkwardly as we wait for traffic to let us cross.

Did I mention that I had sex with Ramie Boulieaux last night? Have you told all of your friends? Go ahead. I can wait.

Traffic clears and we both cross Main Street and head toward Winterhead's town center. Why? I don't know. I have no idea where I'm going. I can barely see straight. There's a sidewalk to my right and cars are passing me on the left. I'm struggling to keep my bike within the eight-inch space between the white line and the sidewalk's curb while sweet and dirty memories course through my body like schools of frantic fish.

Behind me, a car beeps angrily. Looking down, I realize I've veered way out into traffic. Pulling back to the right side of the white line, I stop the bike and pull it up onto the sidewalk.

Nobody walks on these sidewalks, anyway. The car, a spotless silver BMW, speeds off with an impressive squeal.

I keep riding toward downtown Winterhead, dodging over-hanging bushes while images of Ramie's naked body swim through the dirty waters of my mind.

I am the guy your mother warned you about. A barefoot stalker who sneaks into girls' bedroom windows.

And has *sex* with them!

I'm that guy.

But who in goddamn hell was that white tuxedo for? Is Ramie seeing someone on the side? Someone even Jill doesn't know about?

Before I know it, I've wobbled all the way to downtown Winterhead, a cosmopolitan crossroads marked by a gas station, a craft "shoppe," a few restaurants and a Star Market. At this point, I have no idea what to do other than run like hell from my mother, so I stop and pull into the gas station. I ride over to the side of the building by a sour-smelling Dumpster, where no passing cars can see me. Dismounting, I take a few deep breaths. Ramie's full-blown nudity will not fade from the movie screen of my mind. At the corner of the building is a pay phone. Finding no change in Jill's pockets, I decide to commit the unchivalrous act of placing a collect call to her cell phone.

My heart stops beating when she accepts the charges and says, "Where are you?"

"Ramie?"

"Where are you?"

"What did she tell you?" I say.

In the background, I hear Mrs. Boulieaux call out, "Who is it?"

Ramie shouts, "It's Daria."

"Is my—is Jill's mom still there?"

"Jack," she says. "I have to ask you something and you have to promise—"

Footsteps thud toward her; then my mother says, "Is that Daria?"

Into the phone, Ramie says, "Call me if you hear anything, okay? I'll see you tonight, right?"

"Tonight?" I say. "Where?"

In the background, my mother says, "Can I talk to her?"

"Daria?" Ramie says. "Daria?" Then, without hanging up, she says to my mother, "She hung up. She was in the car. But she hasn't seen Jill either."

"Ramie," my mother says. "I can't express to you how important it is that we find Jack."

"Uh-huh," Ramie says.

"If you hear from him," she says, "I need to know right away."

"Uh-huh."

"Why don't you let me hold on to your cell phone. That way, if Jack calls, I can talk to him."

There is a pause. Then Ramie's mother says, "*I'll* hold on to Ramie's cell phone."

I hear Ramie's fingers on the phone; then it disconnects.

I hold the receiver in my hand, hoping she'll return but

knowing she won't. A few feet away, a woman drags a bawling three-year-old from the gas station's little store.

Tonight. Ramie wants me to meet her tonight. I don't even know what day it is. I don't know if I'll still be around tonight.

Leaning my bike against the Dumpster, I head into the store, entry bells a-jingling.

"Hey," I say.

The guy manning the cash register looks up at me, then cringes as his eyes wander to my very thin and very tight orange sweatpants.

"Sorry," I say. "Laundry day."

His eyes continue to descend to my bare feet.

"Yeah," I say. "I know, 'no shirt, no shoes, no service,' but—"

He regards me with unvarnished contempt. I think his name is Brent and I think he dropped out of Winterhead High two years ago.

"Do you know what day it is?" I say.

He smirks at me for a second, takes a swig of Sprite and says, "Saturday," as if I'd have to be mentally compromised not to know that.

"Saturday," I say. But Saturday doesn't mean anything, because I don't know what day it was when I woke up.

"You buying something?" he says.

"Do you know the date?" I say.

With an enormous sigh, he summons every single muscle in his neck to undertake the apparently gargantuan effort of facing the cash register, then says, "Twenty-third."

"June twenty-third?"

"No," he says. "December. You're not gonna try to buy beer from me, right? 'Cause I am definitely carding today."

"Right," I say. "June twenty-third, right?"

He doesn't answer.

"Okay, then," I say. "Thanks."

I take my leave of Brent and return to the smelly Dumpster to parse the data. June 23. That's a solid piece of information. But do I remember the date of Jill's last day? No. I've never paid attention to things like dates, because I am not a calendar nerd like Jill. Not only that, prior to last night's wholly unexpected turn of events, I spent the duration of this phase in an undifferentiated swamp of self-pity with no awareness of how much time was passing.

Wait a minute. June 23? I may not be a calendar nerd, but I remember *that* date. Of course Brent is carding today. Today will be marked by a sudden but not unanticipated increase in the number of minors attempting the illegal purchase of alcohol.

It's Saturday, June 23, people.

Tonight is prom night!

I, Jack McTeague, a.k.a. Ramie Boulieaux's lover, ride at top speed down Grapevine Road en route to the Wilburs' home, where I intend to commit the crime of burglary. Now, I'd like to claim that I have targeted the Wilburs because they're a couple of grasping yuppies who treat their babysitters like servants. That would be a lie. Mr. and Mrs. Wilbur, though rich beyond measure, are the nicest couple around, and their twins were Jill's easiest babysitting gig. No, I am targeting the Wilburs' home for the suits. Mr. Wilbur, if memory serves, was one sharp-dressed M-F. He and his wife would venture out on a Saturday night, dressed to the nines, for dinner "in town." "In town" meant Boston, and Boston meant they'd be gone for at least three hours, giving Jill plenty of time after the twins were asleep to sneak into their walk-in closet to try on Mrs. Wilbur's clothes.

I'm going to the prom, in case you haven't worked it out on your own. Keep up, people. Clock's a-ticking. I don't have time to spoon-feed you. Ramie wants me to meet her "tonight," remember? Tonight is prom night. Need a suit. Get it?

So anyway, I get to the Wilburs' house and stuff my bicycle into a tangle of azalea bushes in the artfully landscaped dividing jungle between their lawn and the Pirellis'.

Did I mention that I made love to Ramie Boulieaux last night? In her bed? And that we were both completely naked the whole time?

Yes?

Good. I want you to be up-to-date.

So anyway. Wilburs' house. Bushes. I'm hunkered down in this miniature amazon with Jill's orange sweatpants sliding so far down my ass that my nuts are getting cold. That, plus the fact that they don't even begin to disguise the outline of my cock, renders them largely irrelevant as clothing, so I decide to peel them off. Someday, one of the twins will venture into these parts in search of a soccer ball, come out with these sweatpants instead and a family mystery will be born.

I am surveying the Wilburs' second-floor master bedroom window, where Mrs. Wilbur appears and disappears in varying stages of dress. Around the front, in their giant curving driveway, sit a Porsche, a Volvo and a Land Rover. The back of the Land Rover is open, and I can hear the twins shouting gaily from somewhere inside.

I squeeze through the bushes, snagging my underwear on a sharp branch, then stay low and move quickly across the lawn to the fringe of bushes rimming the house. Studiously avoiding the noisy gravel bed, I skim the edge of the finely shaped hedge around the corner to the front of the house. Above me, I can hear the twins' frenzied footsteps while Mr. and Mrs. Wilbur call to each other about "the good cooler, not the blue one."

Inching around the oversized hydrangea with its giant bobbing blue heads, I pad over to the ground-level door built into the addition connecting the main house to the garage. Through the screen door, the muted TV plays *The Lion King* for an audience of none. Nudging the screen door open, I step inside.

Upstairs, the twins are momentarily still. "You can take the Ariel or the Belle costume," Mrs. Wilbur says. "Not both."

I peer through the kitchen to the open basement door, which spills yellow light. There's a guest bedroom on the other side of it. Stepping onto the cool black tiles, I tiptoe across the kitchen, catching a glimpse of my half-naked reflection in the large black face of their oven.

Mr. Wilbur's voice drifts up from below. "It's dirty!" he says. "We're taking the blue—"

He cuts himself off and mumbles, "We're taking the blue one. I don't have time for . . ."

I pad quietly past the open basement door as Mr. Wilbur grabs a small blue cooler and turns to head upstairs. Rushing to the guest room, I fumble with the doorknob.

It's locked!

Mr. Wilbur's footsteps thud up the stairs. I'm trapped in the narrow hallway between the basement door and the locked guest room.

I open a door to my right. It's a linen closet, jam-packed. Across the narrow hallway is another door. I open it and slip inside, but there is no time to shut the door before Mr. Wilbur makes it to the top of the stairs. Only an open doorway separates us. All he has to do is turn around to spot me standing in full view in my underwear in the small and, if memory serves, oft-used downstairs bathroom!

He stands inches from me, trying to decipher the whining demands of one of the twins upstairs, then sighs and walks away to put the cooler on the kitchen table.

Trapped now, I slip into the bathtub, where a practically transparent shower curtain would merely blur but not conceal me.

From the sound of things, Mr. Wilbur is loading up the

cooler with lunch from the fridge. A few seconds later, Mrs. Wilbur and the twins clomp down the stairs.

"We've got to get out of here," she says. "They're driving me nuts."

"Daddy, Daddy," one of them says. Then I hear Mr. Wilbur grunt as one of them jumps on him.

None of the Wilburs opts for a last-minute potty visit, and after a few noisy minutes of whining and threats, the whole family is out the door. There is a brief commotion surrounding getting the twins into the Land Rover, followed by the sweet sound of the engine retreating down Grapevine Road.

I step out of the bathtub and sprint upstairs to the master bedroom. The thick carpet absorbs my footsteps as I cross in front of their enormous bed to the walk-in closet, where a bounty of expensive suits awaits me, as does an explosion of dresses, skirts, blouses and shoes that would make Jill and Ramie weep.

By the way, did I mention the oral sex? Yeah, there was oral sex last night too.

So I try on white shirts, blue shirts and shiny silver T-shirts. I try on black shoes and brown shoes, blue ties and yellow ties. Brooks Brothers, Armani, Fendi, D&G. You get the picture. Don't worry. I am not a "vapid label whore" or anything. In fact, I couldn't care less whose name is on the clothes I wear. I just want to look good for my girl.

In all honesty, I can't rule out the possibility that my girl is laying a trap for me. When I arrive at the Karn Beach Yacht

Club tonight, my mother could be waiting with a giant tranquilizer gun.

But I don't think she will be. Maybe it's the delusion of love. Maybe it's the oral sex. I did mention the oral sex, right? Whatever it is, I think Ramie's on my side. There was something in her voice. Something about the way she lied to my mother. At any rate, whether I'm going to the prom or marching straight back to prison, I may as well go in style.

The Wilburs don't return from their day trip. Perhaps the twins have hijacked the Land Rover and are forcing their parents to drive to Disney World at gunpoint.

At eight o'clock, after raiding the fridge and eating the last of their hummus, I suit up in Mr. Wilbur's black D&G suit, shiny black shoes and a white collarless shirt with no tie and mount my ten-speed.

It's only a short trip to Argilla Road, which is little more than a dark three-mile strip with Main Street at one end and Karn Beach Yacht Club at the other. Every few minutes, a car filled with prom goers passes me, two of them marking the occasion by hurling beer cans. Whether I am riding toward my demise or my salvation is unknown. All I know is that Ramie will be there, and this time, I am going to tell her everything.

When I get to the huge gravel parking lot marked by the wooden Karn Beach Yacht Club sign, I do a slow circle of the parking lot. No cop cars. At least, no marked cop cars. And more importantly, Mom's beige Saab is nowhere in sight. Near the entrance is a small herd of rented limos parked at odd angles and listlessly guarded by black-suited men smoking cigarettes.

There's no bike rack, so I lean the bike against the side of the building by a ramp leading to the marina. The faint thud-thud of music drifts from the rear of the building.

A limo pulls up and four kids get out, press their outfits into submission and giggle their way through the main entrance under a green and white striped awning.

I opt for a stealth approach and head toward the music, passing a row of overflowing Dumpsters. About two-thirds of the way back, the artificial brick gives way to floor-to-ceiling windows. I peer inside. Colored lights bouncing off a mirrored ball near the ceiling make a swirling confetti pattern on the wooden dance floor, where a small cluster of girls shimmy together in long pastel dresses. I continue walking to the rear of the building.

Around the corner is another set of Dumpsters and an open door through which a cheap radio tinnily blares metal hits from a bygone era. I press myself up against the doorjamb, but a stack of cardboard boxes blocks the kitchen from view. I can hear the clinking of plates and glasses and the insistent hum of male and female kitchen staff.

I step around the boxes. The busy kitchen staff, all clad in black polyester pants, white shirts and black vests, doesn't seem to notice me. A fortyish guy responds to the ding of a microwave by removing a large tray of mini pizzas. On a stainless steel table are three humongous plastic bowls into which a teenage girl with bad acne pours pineapple juice while next to her an older Hispanic woman slices oranges.

"Yo, can I help you?"

I turn to my left to see a fiftyish man in the same penguin uniform eyeballing me suspiciously.

"Yeah," I say. "I'm here to pick up my little sister."

He squeezes his eyebrows together while tilting his head back, which is the international gesture for "Don't BS me, punk."

"I got a call," I say, "from her friend." Then I lower my voice to a whisper. "She's drunk."

The Hispanic woman cutting oranges makes a clucking sound followed by a singsong sigh. Another waiter, twentyish, crashes through the swinging doors carrying a huge tray crammed with empty plastic cups. "Friggin' losers," he says. "We got another punch bowl down."

The fiftyish guy, who I guess is in charge of the whole classy affair, exhales deeply. "Fabiana," he says. "You and Britney this time."

The Hispanic woman stops cutting oranges and exchanges a look with the girl pouring the pineapple juice; then the two of them head into the function room.

The guy in charge looks at me. "Go ahead."

I make my way around the stainless steel tables and industrial-capacity dishwashers to the swinging doors leading to the function room. Through the round window, I take in the sights. White Grecian columns enwreathed in blue and white crepe paper hold up a few dateless geeks who stare in pointless longing at the girls dancing before, but not *for,* them. In the far corner, a DJ presses one giant headphone to his ear while unsleeving a record album. He too is wearing a cheap black suit. They must all come from the same place.

"Dude, this is a working kitchen. You mind?"

I turn to find a kid around my age carrying one of the humongous punch bowls. I step out of his way.

When he eases through the swinging door, I follow him.

To my continued relief, a giant net does not drop from the ceiling to trap me, nor do paratroopers swing in through the floor-to-ceiling windows bordering the room. I hang back by the punch bowls and survey the scene.

There are about two hundred kids here and maybe fifteen chaperones. Mostly teachers but some parents too. I do not see Mom. I do not see Mrs. Boulieaux. And I do not see any cops.

What I do see is the entire senior class of Winterhead High spiffed up like I've never seen them. Well, I never *have* seen them. Not with my own eyes, anyway. Shelly Doucette and Avina Loman rush by me, sweaty, giggling and trailing an aura of cheap vanilla perfume.

I know most of these kids. And not a single one of them knows I exist.

From the giant bank of speakers, the song segues seamlessly into AC/DC's "You Shook Me All Night Long" and the dance floor bulges with girls who cannot wait to grind themselves against each other. A few tuxedoed guys join the fun, but it's mostly a girl-on-girl affair. Around the perimeter of the dance floor, the guys speak quietly to each other, eyes on their dates and their dates' friends.

Way on the other side of the dance floor, through a tangle of heavily made-up girls with their hair in buns and twists and weird curlicues, I spot Tommy Knutson. He's wearing a black suit jacket and a T-shirt with something written on it in sequins. Definitely gay. I don't care what Jill says. Plus he's talking to some guy in a white tux who has his back to me and is leaning against one of the columns. I wonder if it's his date. As I circle the dance floor to get a better view, the eyeballs of other students begin to stick to me. Especially the eyeballs of girls.

"Hey, Daria," I say.

She stops walking and faces me, then tugs at her black bustier top. "Do I know you?" she says. Her eyes wander down my body and back up again.

I don't answer in time. All six feet four inches of Noah Trainor step in to engulf Daria in his meaty arms. He shoots me a warning scowl, then drags Daria onto the dance floor.

Daria's eyes linger on mine for a second as he pulls her into the swirling throng.

I continue my circle of the dance floor, collecting more eyeballs as I go. As I near Tommy Knutson, I realize the guy in the white tux has long hair piled up on his head like a girl. And when I get far enough around the dance floor to get a full profile, I realize Tommy Knutson is not speaking to a dude in a white tux with a girl's hairdo. He's speaking to Ramie.

So *that's* who the white tux was for.

I duck behind a column, but the suddenness of the move draws Tommy's attention. He scrunches up his face in inquiry, then says something to Ramie. Still leaning against the column, Ramie cranes her neck around to see me. I pull back, but it's too late. She spots me.

Tucked into a corner beneath a crepe paper archway, the DJ, some middle-aged townie trapped in 1985, spins "Tainted Love" to a round of squeals and another swelling of the dance floor.

Tommy says something to Ramie. I can't read lips, but I figure it's something along the lines of "Who's that ass hat hiding behind the column?" Colored lights throb in time with the song's electronic hook as Ramie says something that looks like "I don't know." Then she walks over to me, the white tuxedo clinging like a second skin. Opening in a wide V down the front, it's fringed with ruffles, as if to indicate a standard tuxedo shirt while exposing a torturously wide expanse of smooth vanilla skin. Memories of last night surge through me and I have to cling to the column to remain upright.

"You came," she says.

"Uh-huh."

I know I should be looking around for plainclothes detectives or some other nefarious agent of Mom's wanting to net me like an escaped gorilla, but I can't stop looking at her. Her eyes are shrouded in dark blue, her lips all shiny, and her skin a flawless expanse of milky white.

"You know it's not true, right?" I say.

"What?"

"Whatever Jill's mother told you."

She narrows her eyes at me. "She told me quite a lot."

"Where is she? Why isn't she here?"

Ramie glances around. "She's out looking for you. I told her I'd call if you showed up here."

"None of it's true," I say.

"How do you know what she said?"

"I know her, Ramie. She told you . . . let's see. She told you I was an Esswich kid or . . . no, no, a Lansdale kid, probably. That I'm stalking Jill and that I'm wanted for . . ." I try to conjure the hideous capacity of Mom's mind.

"Murder," Ramie says. "You killed a teacher. In Quebec."

I can't help smiling at that one. "And how exactly did Jill meet me?" I say.

Ramie breathes in deeply. "At the beach last summer."

"Really," I say. "Where she was with *you* almost every day?"

Ramie nods.

"What an amateur," I say. "Jill's safe. She'll be back by tomorrow or the next day at the latest."

Ramie's nostrils flare. "And you know this because?"

"I know this because—" I stop suddenly. Then I touch Ramie's fingers and take her hand in mine. "I know this because I'm her."

Ramie says nothing as she stares at me, her eyes glistening with sudden tears that do not drop.

"I know it's impossible," I say. "But—"

She takes my other hand and pulls me close to her. Bringing her lips softly to mine, she kisses me, then pulls back.

"You believe me?" I say.

She shakes her head.

"You think I'm lying?"

She shakes her head again.

"Ramie—"

"Shhh."

Her left hand finds the small of my back as she shuffles me backward onto the dance floor. Wrapping her fingers around my palm, she begins swaying gently from side to side as her hand climbs my back to rest on my shoulder. Jason Grimby, a few feet to my left, takes a break from feeling up Alison Lambert to sneer inquisitively at me, then loses himself in her sloppy kiss.

When the song segues to its Diana Ross bridge, I pull Ramie close and we begin circling gently, our knees bumping as we shuffle. We are not dancing, exactly. We are merely moving with and against each other, swaying side to side in a sea of swaying kids as if we were both perfectly normal. No one here knows I had sex with Ramie last night. No one here knows my secret. I'm not sure even Ramie has grasped what I've told her. It's as if the heat of her torso pressing against mine has melted away the sordid truth and we're just two ordinary teenagers committing foreplay on the dance floor while an army of chaperones watches helplessly from the perimeter. The ordinariness of it all is nothing short of extraordinary.

Ramie gasps suddenly.

"What?" I say.

I follow her eyes downward. My right arm is shaking.

"What's wrong?" she says.

"Oh no."

I pull her through the clot of undulating taffeta to the edge of the dance floor, but my own legs stop me.

"Jack?" she says.

Tommy Knutson, watching us from the support of a white column, rushes over.

A sharp pain fires from my lower spine and I crumple to the floor.

Ramie drops to her knees with me. "What's happening!" she says.

Tommy Knutson grabs me around the shoulders and helps me up. "Is he drunk?" he says. "Is he going to puke?"

The two of them try to walk me to an exit door a mere ten feet away, but my legs won't work. The pain shoots down my outer thighs. My knees crackle like fireworks, then buckle. I fall to the floor.

A sharp gasp rises from a few kids nearby on the dance floor, but the music keeps playing.

The muscles of my abdomen contract. "Please, no," I say.

Ramie drops to her knees again. "What should we do? Tell me."

"Get me . . ." My voice mutates into a deep groan. "Get . . . me . . . out of here." I start panting.

Ramie slings my arm around her shoulder and tries to pull

me up. In the distance, Mrs. Tosier tries to squeeze through the knot of kids, some of whom are staring at me, some of whom are still dancing.

"I'm serious, Rames," I say. "Get me out of here." A brutal jab attacks my lower spine and I hear myself moan. Ramie calls out to me but her voice gets swallowed up in the music and my own agonized breathing.

Then all sound vanishes.

My back arches, brutally plastering the top of my head to the hard wooden floor. Colored flecks of light spiral around me. Eyes bear down. Ramie's eyes. Tommy's eyes. Mrs. Tosier's eyes. Alison Lambert's and Jason Grimby's eyes. Eyes atop tuxedoed bodies. Eyes atop satin and silk. Eyes beneath sweaty updos.

I am no longer invisible. Their eyes consume me, big, open and full of horror.

The change has begun.

JUNE 23

Jill

Through the murky screen of my eyelashes, the first thing I notice is a bright yellow light coming at me, followed by a pink one and a blue one. Underwater voices murmur indecipherably. Music plays loud and bassy. When I blink, I realize the lights are skipping across a wooden floor. Up above, a shiny reflective globe spins.

"Can you hear me?" someone says. "Jill, can you hear me?"

Other voices resolve from the din. "Wow!" someone says. "Did you see that?"

A blurry round face sitting atop a blur of mauve bears down on me. I stare at it until I recognize it as belonging to Mrs. Tosier, a chubby Spanish teacher I never had. On my other side, a white shape, vaguely humanoid, sits or kneels while colored lights dance across it. As it scoots toward me, I try to make out its details. Angel-like, it kneels at my side, then whisks long fingers down my cheek.

What a strange dream.

I stare into the angel's blurred face until its details become

Ramie's. Behind her in a beautiful green chiffon dress is Alison Lambert, her hands pressed together over her nose.

It must be morning. I close my eyes and wait for the dream to end, wait for wakefulness to claim me. But the voices keep murmuring while footsteps patter and stomp.

I hear music, then the words "ambulance" and "mother."

Then Ramie shouts, "No!"

Sliding her white arm beneath my shoulders, she lifts my liquid torso off the wooden floor. Mrs. Tosier tries to stop her, but Ramie keeps pulling me until I am half standing on limp legs. Repositioning her arms around my waist, she jerks me upright. From the indistinct fringe of people shapes, another shape steps forward. Thrusting its forearms under my armpits, it lifts me up until I am fully standing. My legs stiffen and my knees lock into position.

"Hey," I say. I've endured the surreal logic of early-morning dreams often enough to know that there is no point in resisting them. These two angels want me to stand. That's good enough for me. Perhaps they're flying me out of here, wherever "here" is.

"Ramie," I say to the white angel. "Where are you taking me?"

Both arms firmly around my waist, Ramie leads me away from the colored lights through a sudden parting of the fringe of people shapes. Some of them are dancing. Some of them are staring. A red exit light beams at us. I face the other angel, who holds my right arm firmly.

"Hey," I say. "I know you." It's Tommy Knutson. Judging by his ashen face, he appears to have endured a recent trauma.

"Where are we going?" I say.

He exhales but doesn't answer.

I look out at the crowd of people shapes until they turn into actual people. Samantha Kitteridge, Brenda Weinstein, Mrs. MacLaine from freshman English, Steven Price.

"Hey, Steven," I say.

He doesn't answer.

Everyone's dressed in long gowns or suits. It must be a wedding or . . .

Looking down, I notice that I'm wearing a suit too, a man's suit that is several sizes too big. Two giant black shoes poke out from the hem of my pants. I stare into their shiny facade, then face Ramie. "Why am I wearing this?"

"Shhh," she says. "Let's go outside."

Mrs. Tosier steps forward and grabs Ramie's elbow. "We need to call her parents."

"No," Ramie says. "It's okay. I'm taking her home."

Grabbing me around the waist again, she guides me to the bright red exit light.

Tommy follows us. "Shouldn't we at least *call* her parents?" he says.

"Definitely not," Ramie says.

We emerge from the building under a canvas awning where a cluster of limousines awaits.

"Ramie," I say. "This isn't a dream, is it?"

She guides me past the limousines into the expansive parking lot, which I recognize all too well. At the far end is a large wooden sign and on it are the words "Karn Beach Yacht Club."

"Oh mal," I say.

"Come on," Ramie says. She tugs me between two rows of parked cars.

I have to hold my pants up, and the bottoms keep getting trapped under the big black shoes as we crunch through the gravel of the parking lot. When we get to her Toyota, I almost collapse face-first against the passenger door. Ramie turns me around so that I'm merely leaning against it.

"How do you feel?" she says. "Do you need to sit?" She straightens out my suit and wipes the sweat from my forehead with her sleeve.

I bring the backs of my fingers to my forehead to feel how sweaty I am and realize I'm not wearing my wig. "Ramie," I say. "How did I get here?"

Ramie glances at Tommy, who shakes his head in utter confusion.

I grab Ramie's arm, awaiting both an explanation for and an escape from what I already suspect is a horrifying reality.

"You don't remember?" she says.

But I'm starting to remember. Fragments of someone else's reality are angling into my memory.

Ramie steps even closer and puts both hands on my face. "It's okay," she says. "We'll work it out."

She knows.

She leans closer still and presses her forehead to mine. In the quietest of whispers, she says, "I knew last night."

I yank my head away from her. "What happened last night?"

Tommy steps forward. "Yeah, what happened last night?"

Ramie's eyes burn into me and I cannot look away. The pale oval of my face reflects in her dark brown irises. We remain frozen in each other's gaze, with no information passing.

Until it does.

In fast motion, like a sped-up movie, images of last night flicker through my mind. Ramie's white stomach, her ecstatic face, the writhing, undulating spasms of our impossible union.

"I am . . . ," I say.

"What?" Ramie says.

"All girl." Hinging at the waist, I collapse at Ramie's feet. "Plan B," I groan. "Black dot. Black dot!"

Tommy puts his arms around me. "I've got her." He lifts me to my feet while Ramie opens the door.

"Lay her down in the backseat," she says.

Tommy slides me in, then sits next to me. I discover I'm sitting on something rough. I grab at a bit of black tulle, then pull it gently from underneath me. It's my prom dress.

Ramie gets in the front seat and starts the car.

"The mirror," I say. "I need the mirror!" I reach over the front seat and angle the rearview mirror so that I can see my face. It's sweaty, pale, terrified and topped with a hideous outcropping of sloppy hair spikes. Neverthless, I take it all in. Then I sit back and close my eyes. "I am all girl," I whisper.

"Shouldn't we take her home?" Tommy says.

"Home," I say. "Yes."

"No," Ramie says. "We can't do that."

"I am all girl," I whisper.

"I know," Tommy says. "It's okay."

"I am all girl." I keep searching for the black dot, but it's nowhere to be found. And frames of last night's grotesque Jack-movie keep flickering by. Not just sight but sound and touch. Her voice. My voice. My *Jack*voice. A full picture in three dimensions and all five senses fleshes itself out.

I grit my teeth. "I am . . ."

The car jerks forward and I open my eyes. At the entrance of the club, Mrs. Tosier waddles from beneath the awning, trailing a handful of curious students who stare at us as we drive past.

"I am . . . ," I say.

Tommy puts his arm around me. "Jill?" he says. "Tell me what to do."

I face him. ". . . all girl?"

But it's not working. I drop my head into his lap and pass out.

"I don't trust her, Tommy. Jack was afraid of what she'd do."

"Ramie, hold on. Are you telling me—"

"I've never liked her."

"Yeah, but—"

"You don't understand."

"I know, Ramie. I just—"

"Listen to me, Tommy. The woman is not right."

"I get it."

"I don't think you do."

"Okay, Ramie. Fine. We won't call her mother. *You had sex with Jill last night?*"

"Shhh. I had sex with *Jack* last night."

This time, I know I'm not dreaming. I'm in the back of Ramie's car with my sweaty cheek plastered to the leather seat, my unworn prom dress slung over the front seat.

"But you said you knew it was her," Tommy says.

"Only sort of."

I lift myself up and wipe the drool from my chin. All of the windows are open, and the car is parked at the edge of the woods. Ramie and Tommy stand about twenty feet away, at the shore of Arrowhead Lake.

"What do you mean by 'sort of'?" Tommy says.

They both have their hands in their pockets and their backs to me.

"Subconsciously," Ramie says. "I think."

They're nearly the same height, Ramie in white, Tommy in black.

"There *were* clues," Ramie says.

"There were?"

"Come on, Tommy. The haircut. The scar."

"I don't know anything about a scar," Tommy says. "And I didn't know Jack. He was your mystery window guy, not mine. This is so messed up." Tommy kicks at a rock and it goes skidding into the water.

Ramie grabs his wrist. "Tommy," she says. "You deeply *cannot* freak out."

If I'm very quiet, I could slide out the window and sneak home. It's less than half a mile from here.

"Well, what are we supposed to do?" he says.

"Does it matter?"

I start to squeeze my shoulders through the open window.

"She's passed out in the back of your car, Ramie. We have to do something."

"No," Ramie says. "I mean, does it matter to you? What she is."

Silence. I freeze with the window's edge pressing into my stomach.

"I guess it shouldn't," Tommy says. "But—"

Ramie faces him. "But what?"

Quietly, I slide back into the car.

"Well, what are we supposed to do? Share them?"

Ramie shrugs, then kicks at a stone, which skids a few feet from her. "I don't know, Tommy. But I do know that we can't take her home to her mother."

"Why not?" he says.

"Her mother told me Jack was a murderer."

"Maybe he is."

"She told me he was stalking Jill, which is not physically possible."

"I don't know how any of this is physically possible."

"Neither do I." Ramie crouches and picks up a flat rock. Sidearming it into the lake, she watches it skip twice, then disappear.

Resting my arms on the open window, I let the damp aquatic air cool my face while Ramie and Tommy stare into the black face of the lake without speaking.

Ramie and I used to ride our bikes to Arrowhead Lake in

middle school and pretend we were Indian princesses founding a new tribe, a tribe of two. There were no houses visible from the lake and no one to interfere with us. We told each other everything. We kept no secrets. Her name was Skipping Rock. Mine was Swooping Dragonfly.

"Maybe we should wake her up," Tommy says.

"No," Ramie says. "Let her sleep for a while."

Through four years of high school I have lived a lie, never realizing, until now, just how lonely that was.

But high school is over. The lie is dead. There's only one thing left to do.

I pull the door handle and Ramie and Tommy face me in perfect synchronicity. Ramie starts to walk over, but I hold up my hand. Opening the door, I get out and stand on my own two wobbly legs.

"You feel okay?" she says.

As I walk toward them, I'm about to say that I feel like a catastrophe still unfolding, but those words seem inadequate.

"You look good," Ramie says. "I mean, the suit's a bit Annie Hall, maybe."

I stand between them and finger the lapel of the suit. "D and G," I say. "I think Jack stole this from Mr. Wilbur."

"The twins' dad?" Ramie says.

I nod.

She looks at me for a few seconds; then we both stare at the lake, its smooth black surface spread out into a near-perfect circle.

The black dot, at last.

But I no longer seek its oblivion. For the moment, anyway, I am content to stand here at the edge, knowing that what comes next is beyond my control.

I let my fingers touch the back of Tommy's hand. He starts at first, then wraps his warm fingers around mine. When he's summoned the courage to do so, he pulls his hypnotic brown eyes from the lake and lays them right on me. This time I don't count.

I can feel Ramie watching us, noticing our hands. She wants to reach out to me, but for once, she's waiting for me to take the lead.

I touch the lapel of Tommy's suit. "What does your shirt say?"

He pulls the jacket open, revealing a navy blue T-shirt with the words "Prom Is for Losers" written in glitter.

"Nice," I say. I hold on to his hand, and when I've summoned the courage to do so, I reach my other hand back toward Ramie. Without any hesitation, she takes it with long cool fingers.

"So," I say. "Are you ready for the truth and nothing but the truth?"

They both look at me and nod.

"You're sure?"

"Yes," Tommy says.

"Born ready," Ramie says.

"All right," I say.

And then I begin.

LAUREN MCLAUGHLIN grew up in a small Massachusetts town called Wenham. She had a normal, crisis-free upbringing, which has utterly deprived her of personal horror stories from which to draw for her fiction. The parents in *Cycler* are very definitely not based on her own parents.

After college and a short stint in graduate school, she spent ten "unglamorous" years in the film industry, both writing and producing, before abandoning her screen ambitions to write fiction full-time. *Cycler* is her first published novel and she is currently working on the sequel.

Lauren is passionate about writing, women's rights, and technology. She lives with her photographer husband, Andrew Woffinden, in Brooklyn. Her Web site and blog can be found at www.laurenmclaughlin.net.